Honeydale

Annabelle Starr

EGMONT

Special thanks to:

Sarah Delmege, St John's Walworth Church of England
School and Belmont Primary School

EGMONT
We bring stories to life

Published in Great Britain 2007
by Egmont UK Limited
239 Kensington High Street, London W8 6SA

Text & illustration © 2007 Egmont UK Ltd
Text by Sarah Delmege
Illustrations by Helen Turner

The moral rights of the author and illustrator have been asserted

ISBN 978 1 4052 3246 3

3 5 7 9 10 8 6 4 2

A CIP catalogue record for this title is available
from the British Library

Typeset by Avon DataSet Ltd, Bidford on Avon, Warwickshire
Printed and bound in Great Britain by the CPI Group

'I like a bit of a mystery, so I thought it was very good'
Phoebe, age 10

'I liked the way there's stuff about modelling and
make-up, cos that's what girls like'
Beth M, age 11

'Great idea – very cool! Not for boys . . .'
Louise, age 9

'I really enjoyed reading the books. They keep
you on your toes and the characters are really interesting
(I love the illustrations!) . . . They balance out humour
and suspense'
Beth R, age 10

'Exciting and quite unpredictable. I like that the girls
do the detective work'
Lauren, age 10

'All the characters are very realistic. I would definitely
recommend these to a friend'
Krystyna, age 9

We want to know what *you* think about
Megastar Mysteries! Visit:

www.mega-star.co.uk

for loads of coolissimo megastar
stuff to do!

Meet the
Megastar Mysteries Team!

Hi, this is me, **Rosie Parker** (otherwise known as Nosy Parker), and these are my best mates . . .

. . . **Soph** (Sophie) **McCoy** – she's a real fashionista sista – and . . .

. . . **Abs** (Abigail) **Flynn**, who's officially une grande genius.

Here's my mum, **Liz Parker**.
Much to my embarrassment,
her fashion and music taste
is well and truly stuck in the
1980s (but despite all that
I still love her dearly) . . .

. . . and my nan,
Pam Parker, the murder-
mystery freak I mentioned
on the cover. Sometimes,
just sometimes, her crackpot
ideas do come in handy.

Consider yourself introduced!

ROSIE'S MINI MEGASTAR PHRASEBOOK

Want to speak our lingo, but don't know your soeurs from your signorinas? No problemo! Just use my comprehensive guide . . .

-a-rama	add this ending to a word to indicate a large quantity: e.g. 'The after-show party was celeb-a-rama'
amigo	Spanish for 'friend'
au contraire, mon frère	French for 'on the contrary, my brother'
au revoir	French for 'goodbye'
barf/barfy/barfissimo	sick/sick-making/very sick-making indeed
bien sûr, ma soeur	French for 'of course, my sister'
bon	French for 'good'
bonjour	French for 'hello'
celeb	short for 'celebrity'
convo	short for 'conversation'
cringe-fest	a highly embarrassing situation
Cringeville	a place we all visit from time to time when something truly embarrassing happens to us
cringeworthy	an embarrassing person, place or thing might be described as this
daggy	Australian for 'unfashionable' or unstylish'
doco	short for 'documentary'
exactamundo	not a real foreign word, but a great way to express your agreement with someone
exactement	French for 'exactly'

excusez moi	French for 'excuse me'
fashionista	'a keen follower of fashion' – can be teamed with 'sista' for added rhyming fun
glam	short for 'glamorous'
gorge/gorgey	short for 'gorgeous': e.g. 'the lead singer of that band is gorge/gorgey'
hilarioso	not a foreign word at all, just a great way to liven up 'hilarious'
hola, señora	Spanish for 'hello, missus'
hottie	no, this is *not* short for hot water bottle – it's how you might describe an attractive-looking boy to your friends
-issimo	try adding this ending to English adjectives for extra emphasis: e.g. coolissimo, crazissimo – très funissimo, non?
je ne sais pas	French for 'I don't know'
je voudrais un beau garçon, s'il vous plaît	French for 'I would like an attractive boy, please'
journos	short for 'journalists'
les Français	French for, erm, 'the French'
Loserville	this is where losers live, particularly evil school bully Amanda Hawkins
mais	French for 'but'
marvelloso	not technically a foreign word, just a more exotic version of 'marvellous'
massivo	Italian for 'massive'
mon amie/mes amis	French for 'my friend'/'my friends'
muchos	Spanish for 'many'

non	French for 'no'
nous avons deux garçons ici	French for 'we have two boys here'
no way, José!	'that's never going to happen!'
oui	French for 'yes'
quelle horreur!	French for 'what horror!'
quelle surprise!	French for 'what a surprise!'
sacré bleu	French for 'gosh' or even 'blimey'
stupido	this is the Italian for 'stupid' – stupid!
-tastic	add this ending to any word to indicate a lot of something: e.g. 'Abs is braintastic'
très	French for 'very'
swoonsome	decidedly attractive
si, si, signor/signorina	Italian for 'yes, yes, mister/miss'
terriblement	French for 'terribly'
une grande	French for 'a big' – add the word 'genius' and you have the perfect description of Abs
Vogue	it's only the world's most influential fashion magazine, darling!
voilà	French for 'there it is'
what's the story, Rory?	'what's going on?'
what's the plan, Stan?	'which course of action do you think we should take?'
what the crusty old grandads?	'what on earth?'
zut alors!	French for 'darn it!'

Hi Megastar reader!

My name's Annabelle Starr*. I'm a fashion stylist – just like Soph's Aunt Penny – which means it's my job to help celebrities look their best at all times.

Over the years, I've worked with all sorts of big names, some of whom also have seriously big egos! Take the time I flew all the way to Japan to style a shoot for a girl band. One of the members refused to wear the designer number I'd picked out for her and insisted on sporting a dress her mum had run up from some revolting old curtains instead. The only way I could get her to take it off was to persuade her it didn't match her pet Pekinese's outfit!

Anyway, when I first started out, I never dreamt I'd write a series of books based around my crazy celebrity experiences, but that's just what I've done with Megastar Mysteries. Rosie, Soph and Abs have just the sort of adventures I wish my friends and I could have got up to when we were teenagers!

I really hope you enjoy reading the books as much as I enjoyed writing them!

Love **Annabelle**

* I'll let you in to a little secret: this isn't my real name, but in this business you can never be too careful!

Chapter One

I still couldn't believe it. Me, Rosie Parker, on my way to London to be a journalist – a JOURNALIST! – on *Star Secrets* magazine. It was only the best mag in the country, if not the universe. Basically, it was the bestissimo thing since cheesy chips, with brilliant features, quizzes, fashion and, most importantly, the most fantasticissimo celebrity interviews. And I was going to work on it. I mean, that could be it – my big break. I could become the best celebrity writer they'd ever had. I could end up a totally famous writer with loads of cool celebrity friends, who'd all give speeches about how they'd never have made it without me. And a film company would make a movie of my life and huge stars like Hilary Duff and Lindsay Lohan would fight over who got to play me. OK, so neither Hilary nor Lindsay had birds' nests masquerading for hair, or one annoying bit of eyebrow which permanently stuck out at a très attractive 90-degree angle from their head, no matter what they try, but hey, it was my movie. Oooh, I could just see the gossip columns:

LATEST GOSSIP JUST IN!

Which famous film star had a near miss when another A-lister poured champagne over her at a star-studded celebrity party? The attacker refused to apologise. 'She deserved it,' she told shocked fellow diners. 'She's landed the part of Rosie Parker. It's only the biggest role in film history!' Upon hearing this, five other female stars had to be restrained from bashing the victim over the head with their It-bags.

My mobile beeped, snapping me back to the present. Oooh, text message from Abs:

> **Still can't believe me and Soph r stuck in Bore-ing-hurst while u have wk's work experience on Star Secrets. We'll miss U!! X :-(**

OK, OK, so maybe I was getting a little carried away. It wasn't like this was a permanent job. But then I'm only 14 – there are laws against children working full-time, y'know. Work-experience slots on *Star Secrets* are like gold dust – seriously, they're rarer than Simon Cowell's compliments. It says in the front of the magazine that there aren't any available for the next two years, so there's no point ringing up trying to get one. So how did I manage to swing it? Well, basically *Star Secrets* ran a competition to write a story and the prize was not only to have the winning story published in – yep, you guessed it – *Star Secrets*, but also a week's work experience. I couldn't believe it when I got the phone call to say I'd won. Literally couldn't believe it. In fact, I made a bit of an idiot of myself. The conversation went something like this:

Me: *Hello.*

Woman's voice: *Hi. Could I speak to Rosie Parker, please?*

Me: *Speaking.*

Woman's voice: *Hi, Rosie. This is Belle Clarkson, editor of* Star Secrets.

Me: *Yeah, right.*

Woman's voice: *Er, sorry?*

Me: *If you're Belle Clarkson, I'm the sixth member of Girls Aloud.*

Woman's voice: *Rosie, I can assure you, I am Belle Clarkson.*

Me: *Look, I know it's you, Amanda Hawkins. If it isn't enough that you already made an idiot of me at school today by pointing out to the whole class that I had a massivo streamer of toilet roll attached to my shoe, now you're trying to torment me in the* *evenings, too. Well, it's about time you got yourself a life. Why don't you just go back to Loserville with all your loser friends and get lost?*

Woman's voice: *Um, right. Rosie? Look, I'm really not Amanda, um, Dorkins, was it?*

Me: *[starting to giggle] Dorkins? Dorkins? As in dork? That's hilarious! I think another school nickname might just have been born. But hang on a minute – if you're not Amanda Dork-Hawkins, that means you really are . . .*

Woman's voice: *Belle Clarkson, Editor of* Star Secrets.

OOPS!

Fortunately, Belle saw the funny side. In fact, she said I'd made her day, although she might have changed her mind after I screamed at the top of my lungs when she told me I'd won the competition. Not only would my story be published in one of the April issues of *Star Secrets*, but my work experience was fixed for school half-term!

So that's why I was now pulling my suitcase off the luggage shelf as the train pulled into London Waterloo, accidentally hitting the woman in front of me on the head in my rush. To say that I was totally excited would be a bit of an under-statement.

Penny was waiting for me by the ticket barrier, looking totally amazing in skinny jeans, black knee-high boots and a battered grey leather jacket. Penny is my best friend Soph's aunt, and basically the coolest person *ever*, and I was staying at her flat for the week. She's a fashion stylist and totally knows EVERYONE worth knowing – including loads of celebs. Penny gets to hang out with famous people all the time. But, like the professional she is, she never gets star-struck. Which, when you think about it, is probably a very good thing. I mean, just imagine if you were styling a huge star, like Madonna, and you got a fit of nerves just as you were doing up her dress, and you ended up breaking the zip and having to cut her out? Talk about embarrassing! Anyway, Penny says most celebs are just ordinary, decent people who happen to have amazing lives.

As soon as she spotted me, she ran forward and gave me a massive hug. 'Rosie! You look fab. How are you?'

Without waiting for an answer, she ushered me out of the station and towards the main road, talking nineteen to the dozen.

'It's so great to have you here again,' she said, stepping into the road and expertly flagging down a passing taxi, much to the annoyance of everyone who was patiently queuing in the taxi rank on the other side of the street. You could so tell who Soph took after in her family. Ignoring the disgruntled shouts of 'Oi, there's a queue here,' and 'Who does she think she is?' Penny hustled me into the taxi and, giving the driver her address, leant back into the seat to give me her full attention.

'I can't wait to hear all your news. And I can't believe you won a week's work experience on *Star Secrets*. That's totally amazing!' she said. 'I bet Soph and Abs are greener than frogs with travel sickness! It's such a shame you couldn't all come; it would have been great fun.'

The original plan had been for me, Abs and Soph to stay all week. We'd all stayed once before when Penny had swung us jobs as runners on the film set where Paige and Shelby Sweetland, the famous Australian celebrity twins, were making their latest movie. But Soph had been given extra shifts at Dream Beauty, the salon where she had a Saturday job, which meant she couldn't make it. Then Abs's Aunt Stacey (she's nowhere *near* as cool as Penny – well, not unless sensible shoes, kilts and hand-knitted jumpers have suddenly become the height of fashion) rang and said she was visiting from Canada. Of course, Abs's parents wouldn't hear of her not being there to see her, so that left little old me.

'I hope you don't mind, but my friend Sally is coming round for dinner tonight. I couldn't cancel. She's a make-up artist on that soap *Honeydale*, which means she's been working flat out and I haven't seen her for ages.'

'*Honeydale*?' I sat bolt upright, staring at Penny in amazement. 'Are you *serious*?'

'Yup,' Penny nodded, grinning at me as soon as she saw the look on my face.

'I LOVE *Honeydale* – it's my favourite soap. I never miss an episode! I can't *believe* you know someone who works on it.'

'So I'm guessing you don't mind that Sally's coming over for dinner, then?' Penny said, smiling and rifling around in her bag for her purse as the taxi pulled up outside her building. I was practically skipping with excitement as I clambered out. Could this week get any better?

As Penny unlocked the front door, her mobile started ringing. 'Make yourself at home,' she said, flicking open her phone. 'I won't be a mo.'

I love Penny's flat. It's exactly the kind of place I dream of living in when I'm older, earning loads of money as a mega-successful writer. Everything's cream, which may sound boring, but Penny's added funky cushions, curtains and the most amazing paintings to give it splashes of colour. But the bestissimo thing about Penny's flat is her walk-in wardrobe. As a stylist, Penny's always being given loads of free stuff – cast-offs donated from the celebrities she styles, freebies from designers who are desperate for her to dress celebs in their stuff . . . Basically, she gets sent so many free products and so much make-up she could start her own shop. I'm not joking. The amount of stuff in her wardrobe is dizzying. I mean, literally.

Soph said the first time she saw the flat, just after Penny had moved in, she opened the wardrobe door to reveal shelf after shelf of neatly stacked tops and jumpers, and rows of skirts, trousers, coats, shoes and boots. After staring for a long time, Soph said, 'I think I might faint.' I'm not kidding. She had to sit down on the floor with her head between her knees and breathe deeply for about five minutes. See? Seriously dizzy-making.

I flopped down on one of the two huge, squishy sofas in the lounge. A few minutes later, Penny wandered in, looking annoyed.

'That was Sally on the phone. She's not coming tonight. She's still at the studio and says she's going to have to work late.' She plonked herself down on to the sofa next to me. 'This is the fourth time she's let me down now. I'm torn between feeling completely irritated and worrying about her. We always used to meet up at least once a week for a good old gossip, but since she's started on *Honeydale* I've hardly seen her – she's lost loads of weight and is totally stressed.'

'Oh, no!' I said. 'That's a shame.' I meant it, too – I had been looking forward to hearing all the gossip about *Honeydale*. I bet Sally knew all the latest soap stories and I couldn't wait to hear what all the stars were really like. Especially Cassie St Claire, who was, like, the biggest soap star ever in soap history. Seriously, I bet even the Pope had heard of her!

Penny smiled at me, 'Not to worry. It means we can have a nice evening together, plus you should get an early night – after all, it's your first day at *Star Secrets* tomorrow, don't forget!'

Yeah, right. As if I was ever going to forget that!

Chapter Two

The next day, I set my alarm two hours earlier than I actually had to leave Penny's flat for the *Star Secrets* office. Getting up so early is seriously unheard of for me. Mum pretty much has to hire a brass band to march through my bedroom just to get me to open one eye in the morning. I'm not joking! But today I had a lot of seriously important stuff to do – like choosing what to wear for a start.

One hour and literally ten outfit-changes later, I finally had my clothes for the day sorted:

Skinny jeans
Gold ballet pumps
Top (made by Soph)

Actually, all my outfit choices for the week had been put together on the advice of Soph. To be honest, I'd have much preferred to be in my comfiest pair of jeans and my scruffiest pair of trainers. But, as Soph pointed out (only about a zillion times, I might add), the girls who worked at *Star Secrets* were likely to be complete and utter fashionista sistas. Basically, if I wanted to fit in, I was going to have to make a bit more of an effort on the clothes front.

Soph is always the most originally dressed out of all of us. While everyone else at school is wearing stuff from the high street, Soph's always the one in a top she bought for fifty pence from the local charity shop. She calls it vintage. Personally, I call it wearing someone else's manky old cast-offs, but each to their own.

I checked out my outfit in the mirror. I looked

pretty good, even if I did say so myself. I just hoped everyone at *Star Secrets* would think so too. I don't mind admitting, I was feeling totally, horribly, tum-churningly nervous. My stomach felt like I'd accidentally swallowed a bumper bag of butterflies. Plonking myself down on my bed, I rifled through my bag until I found the list of things Abs and Soph had given me, telling me what *not* to do during my first day at *Star Secrets*. They'd drawn it up to try and stop me from making an idiot of myself during my week on the magazine:

Abs' and Soph's top ten list of things not to do on your first day at *Star Secrets* magazine:

1. Decide wearing your pants on your head is a huge fashion-forward trend that everyone should follow. (Especially if those pants are your old, cringe-tastic days-of-the-week ones!)

2. Not look where you're going and end up traipsing dog poo all through *Star Secrets* swanky offices.

3. Forget everyone's names as soon as they introduce themselves and spend the whole day calling everyone 'sweetie', 'dah-ling', or 'gorgeous'.

4. Run up to the editor and start gushing about how much you love her work, then throw yourself at her feet and beg her to give you a job.

5. Wear heels so high that you only manage to walk about five steps before tripping over and landing head first at the feet of your new boss.

6. Gorge yourself on a family-sized bar of choccie and end up being violently sick all over the fashion editor's très expensive shoes!

7. Listen to your MP3 player while you're working and start singing along out loud and extremely off-key – not realising that every-one in the office is staring at you in horror.

8. Wander into the loos and start doing your business when you suddenly hear a man's voice and realise that you've accidentally gone into the men's by mistake.

9. Take a homemade lunch to work and end up munching away on a pongy egg sandwich while everyone else is having a posh sushi for lunch!

10. Answer the phone and get so flustered you give your name as Snoozy Barker and accidentally call the mag *Strop Secrets!*

Even after reading the list through from start to finish five times, I still felt really nervous about walking into the office. I mean, the last job I had was being a runner on that film set – that mostly involved getting people brekkie and hot drinks, and I'd had Abs and Soph to help. This was real work and I really, *really* didn't want to make an idiot of myself. I decided I should just have a tiny practice at greeting people.

'Hi, I'm Rosie.' I smiled at my reflection.

Not bad, but maybe I should be a bit more chatty.

'Hi, pleased to meet you. I'm Rosie. I can't wait to work with you. I love *Star Secrets* magazine!'

Nope, too over-the-top.

Hmmm.

'I'm Rosie. Good to meet you. See you later. Ciao!' I leant in and pretended to air-kiss the mirror.

'Er, Rosie?' Penny was standing in the doorway behind me, a cup of chocolate in her hand. 'What are you doing?'

'Um . . . just, er, cleaning the mirror. It had, um, a smudge on it,' I said, starting to wipe the mirror frantically with my sleeve, feeling my face go pinker than a baboon's bum.

'If you say so,' Penny said with a smile. 'Anyway, I've got to leave for work, so I just wanted to give you this.' She put the hot chocolate down on the dressing table. 'And I wanted to make sure you knew the way to the tube station.'

'Turn right out of house, follow the road to the

end, turn right at the end, take the first right and the tube station's at the end of the road on the left,' I recited. 'Then take the Piccadilly Line to Piccadilly Circus.'

'Fab,' Penny smiled, giving me a big hug. 'Good luck today. I'll make something special for dinner tonight to celebrate your first day.'

I smiled back at her, 'Thanks – and, er, you really don't have to worry about cooking anything, honestly.' Penny's cooking skills left a lot to be desired, believe me. As my nan would say, she could burn water.

She paused in the doorway and looked me up and down. 'You look totally cool, by the way. Knock 'em dead!'

* * *

An hour later, I stepped out of Piccadilly Circus tube station and made my way to the *Star Secrets* office. It was five minutes away, tucked down a side street, and I couldn't help staring into every shop window I passed. I felt so excited. That's the thing about London – even though the shops are exactly the same as the ones back in Bore-ing-hurst, they just seem so much more exciting. Mad but true.

I walked into the building where the *Star Secrets* office was based. A security guard was sitting behind the reception desk and got me to write my name, who I was there to see and the time I'd arrived in a book, before giving me a visitor's pass (which, let me tell you, I am sooo keeping for the rest of my life, not to mention flashing under Amanda Dork-Hawkins' nose the moment I get back to school). Then he told me to take the lift up to the third floor.

Some girls passed me and stepped into the lift before me. I squeezed in just as the doors closed. They were all super-trendy: one had a bag that Soph had been pointing out in fashion mags and hankering after for I don't know how long, and another had bright yellow nail varnish.

'Which floor?' the bag girl asked me.

'Third,' I said.

'Same as us,' she smiled. 'Love your top.'

'Thanks,' I smiled back.

I followed the girls out of the lift and into a huge room which was painted bright yellow. There was a huge *Star Secrets* sign on one of the walls and what seemed like hundreds of framed *Star Secrets* covers hanging underneath it. A metal spiral staircase stood in the corner. Next to that were some shelves where copies of the mag were neatly arranged, including one which wasn't even out in the shops yet! Oooh, la, la! I wandered over for a closer look.

'Can I help you?' said a voice. I spun round to find the receptionist watching me through narrow eyes. She was wearing a gorgeous pink cardie and her hair was drawn back off her face with a chic hairband. She was also wearing one of those headsets that pop stars wear when they're on stage. As I walked towards her, she held up one perfectissimo manicured finger and started talking into the microphone/receiver/whatever:

'*Star Secrets*, can I help you?' She listened for a moment. 'Putting you through. Hold the line please.' She looked up at me. 'Yes?'

'Um, I'm Rosie Parker – I, er, won a competition and I'm here to do work experience.'

Without taking her eyes off me, she tapped a number into a keypad and spoke into her headset again. I wondered if she sometimes pretended to be a huge megastar like Madonna, on stage singing to thousands of fans. I knew I wouldn't have been able to help myself if I'd had one of those.

'I have a Rosie Parker in reception,' the receptionist was saying. 'OK.'

'Take a seat,' she nodded at a huge blue sofa behind me. 'Someone will be here to collect you in a moment.'

I'd just perched myself on the edge of the sofa when there was a huge clattering noise. I looked up to see a tiny girl in the highest pair of heels *ever* making her way down the metal staircase. Seriously, they were so high, I don't know how she managed to take one step in them, let alone navigate her way down a staircase. I mean, if I'd been wearing them, I'd have fallen head over heels down the metal stairs and ended up sprawled across the *Star Secrets* reception area with my head in the lap of the seriously unimpressed receptionist.

'Rosie?' the girl said, peering over the rail. 'Hi, I'm Suze. I'm the editorial assistant at *Star Secrets*. Belle's sent me to take you up to see her.'

I followed her back up the metal staircase which led into the main office itself. Glancing around, I was glad I had listened to Soph about my outfit, as the office was full of ultra-trendy girls (and a few guys) who all looked like they'd just stepped out of the fashion pages of the magazine. The office was full of chatter and laughter, and music was blaring out of a stereo balanced on top of a filing cabinet. I followed Suze past a row of desks to a smaller office on the right. She paused and knocked on the door.

'Hi, Belle. I have Rosie Parker for you,' she said, stepping aside and pushing me forward into the room. I couldn't help but gawp. The office was bigger than my bedroom at home. It had a huge desk, with a laptop and pages and pages from the magazine printed out all over it. Two huge sofas faced each other in the middle of the room, with a coffee table in between.

'I'm Belle – not to be confused with Amanda Witchface Hawkins!' said Belle. 'It's a pleasure to meet you, Rosie!'

Argghhhhh! I could feel myself blushing as I took her outstretched hand. 'I . . . I . . . I'm so excited to actually be here. I . . . I sooo love *Star Secrets*!' I stammered, sounding like a total idiot.

I knew what Belle looked like, having seen her picture next to the Editor's Letter every week in *Star Secrets*, but she was even more beautiful close up. In fact, Belle Clarkson totally looked like a film star. She was wearing fitted trousers, a loose smock top and her long red hair was tied loosely off her face. I quickly closed my mouth, which was hanging open in a très unattractive goldfishy manner.

'Sit down, sit down.' Belle ushered me to one of the sofas before sticking her head out of the door.

'Candy? Have you got a minute?'

An incredibly glam girl dressed in skinny jeans, heels and a floral mini dress stood up from her computer and walked over to Belle's office.

'What's up?' she said with a friendly grin.

'This is Candy,' said Belle. 'She's *Star Secrets'* features editor and will be looking after you this week. Candy, this is Rosie.'

'Rosie!' Candy beamed at me. 'It's great to meet you. We're very excited about having you here. Your story totally rocked.'

'Thanks!' I blushed some more. Honestly, my face must have been giving off practically the same amount of heat as the sun.

WAY TO LOOK COOL, ROSIE!

'Come and meet the rest of the team,' she smiled.

Belle nodded and winked at me. 'Have fun, Rosie. I'll make sure I catch up with you later.'

Candy led me over to where she'd been sitting earlier. 'Right, you're sitting here, next to Pete, who's our senior writer.'

He looked up and smiled. He was dark and skinny, with brown sticky-up hair, baggy jeans, trainers and a T-shirt that said, 'Welcome to the Dark Side'. Several bracelets were twined round his wrist and he wore at least three chunky rings. Definitely, *definitely* C.U.T.E. – Soph would LOVE him.

'Hey,' he smiled.

'Hi,' I smiled back.

'I sit here,' Candy pointed at the desk opposite Pete's. 'And opposite you is Alice – our junior writer.' She nodded at a girl with long dark hair, who was wearing baggy jeans and an 'I ♥ Shopping' T-shirt.

'Hi,' I smiled. 'I'm Rosie.'

Alice looked up. 'Hiya,' she said. 'Good to have you on board.'

'I've got to run to a meeting,' said Candy, 'so settle yourself in. Pete and Alice will show you where everything is, and later on I'll talk you through exactly what you'll be helping us with this week.'

'OK,' I said, sitting down next to Pete, who grinned at me. He slid back his chair. 'Love your top,' he said. 'Hey, Lolly, have you checked out Rosie's top?'

A flash of silver caught my eye as a girl made her way over to us. She was wearing a pink boiler suit tucked into silver knee-high boots. Her fringe was bright blue, which matched her blue glitter eye shadow. On anyone else the outfit would have looked, well, stupido, basically, but somehow on this girl it just worked.

'This is Lauren, our fashion editor,' he said, 'but everyone calls her Lolly. Lolly, this is Rosie.'

'Hi, Rosie,' she smiled. 'Now, that top is *cool*. Where did you get it?'

'My friend made it,' I managed, smiling back. *Thanks, Soph!*

'Well, your friend's got serious talent,' said Lolly, fingering the hem.

SOPH IS GOING TO WET HERSELF WITH EXCITEMENT WHEN SHE HEARS THIS. THE FASHION EDITOR OF *STAR*

SECRETS MAGAZINE THINKS SHE'S TALENTED!!

✳ ✳ ✳

The day whizzed by. I answered readers' letters and even had a go at writing a quiz. Just as I was packing up my bag, ready to leave, Candy came over to talk to me.

'Thanks for today, Rosie,' she smiled. 'You've been great. Just to let you know, tomorrow and on Wednesday you'll be going to the set of the soap *Honeydale* with Pete and Alice, to help them with an exclusive behind-the-scenes piece they're doing. Come here as usual first thing tomorrow so we can discuss who's doing what, but then you'll be getting a taxi over to the studio with them. Is that OK with you?'

OK? OK???????!!!!!!!!!!!!!! I wanted to get up and cartwheel round the office, shouting, 'I'M GOING TO *HONEYDALE!* I'M GOING TO *HONEYDALE!!*' at the top of my voice!!!

Instead, I nodded and smiled in a calm,

professional manner, as if I was totally asked to go behind the scenes of the country's biggest soap every day. 'Yes, of course – that's fine, Candy.'

'I can't believe you're going to *Honeydale* tomorrow, that's amazing!' said Penny later that night, as we sat in front of the TV, finishing off two humongous pizzas. (True to her previous form as a hideous cook, Penny's attempt to make something special had, not surprisingly, gone horrendously wrong, so she'd resorted to a takeaway – much to my relief!) 'I'll let Sally know, so she can look out for you.'

She reached for her mobile and started texting. I stared into space. I couldn't believe I was going to *Honeydale* either. Seriously, it was, like, the best soap ever. Me, Soph and Abs love it. We spend as many hours talking about the show as we do watching it. I'm always scouring the Internet to try and find out what's going to happen next. And I was actually going to meet

Cassie St Claire. Talk about coolissimo! I was, like, her biggest fan in the world. Seriously, I'd read every single article that had ever been written about her. And now I'd get to meet her in the flesh – not to mention actually see where *Honeydale* is filmed. I mean, just thinking about it, I could get spotted by one of the producers, who'd take one look at me and realise that the soap was crying out for a fourteen-year-old with bird's nest hair and unruly eyebrows and offer me a part on the spot. And Cassie St Claire would take me under her wing, and the two of us would become so close we'd be like sisters . . .

Penny's phone beeped, snapping me back into the present. She picked it up, rolled her eyes, then threw it back on the sofa in irritation.

'Sally says she'll do her best, but she can't promise anything as she's so busy,' Penny scowled. 'Honestly, I feel like I hardly know her since she started on *Honeydale* – she's totally changed. All this stress and weight-loss isn't like her. To be honest, I'm a bit worried about her.'

I decided I'd keep an eye out for Sally on the set the next day so I could reassure Penny that her friend was OK.

Chapter Three

The next morning, after a quick meeting with Candy at the *Star Secrets* office, Pete, Alice and I jumped into a taxi that was now drawing up outside Ridley Studios, where Honeydale is filmed. As senior writer, Pete would be interviewing Cassie St Claire and the other big stars, while Alice would be getting the low-down on what a typical day on set was like, and I was going to be helping her. We were going back the following day with the photographer to make sure we got all the photos that were needed to go with the feature. I was so excited I could hardly sit still.

The car drew up at the kerb and we all clambered out. Outside the entrance were a group of photographers, clicking away and shouting, 'Over 'ere! Over 'ere!' and 'Give us a smile, love!' I stood on tiptoe to get a better look. It had to be one of the stars of *Honeydale*, turning up for a day's filming. Who was it? *Who was it?*

Ooh, la, la! It was the new teenage star of *Honeydale*, Wendy Reed, who played Rosie Lynn – the young tearaway who was breaking hearts and bones all over the soap. Me, Abs and Soph love her almost as much as Cassie St Claire – and here she was! I couldn't believe it. She was walking towards the studio entrance looking totally coolisimo, dressed in jeans, a pink sweatshirt and trainers, with a baseball cap pulled down over her face. Her pet Chihuahua, Tiny, was tucked under her arm.

I could hear the cries of the photographers. 'This way, love. Give us a smile!' And 'Wendy, what's going to happen to Rosie next?'

This was sooo cool! I couldn't wait to meet her. Whenever I'd seen her interviewed, I'd always felt we'd have a lot in common, and not just cos her character had the same first name as me. I just *knew* we would become best friends and Wendy would end up doing interviews on how my friendship was the secret of her success. And there'd be picture after picture of us, caught unawares with our arms slung round each other, laughing our heads off, or of our heads close together, having what was obviously a private heart to heart. And everyone who read the interviews or saw the pictures would know immediately that I was the kind of girl who could see way past celebrity to the person beyond, and girls all over the world would sigh and wish they had a best friend like me.

I was determined to speak to her. I hurried along the pavement and arrived at the door at the same time as her. The cameras were all still clicking away. Ooh, I'd be in all the magazines in the same photo as a soap star! *Just wait until Abs and Soph hear about this.*

'Hi,' I said casually. 'My name's Rosie, too – isn't that a coincidence?'

She looked at me as if I was a complete idiot. 'My name's Wendy. Rosie isn't real,' she said in a voice blistering with scorn (call me paranoid, but I could have sworn even her dog, Tiny, gave me a dirty look), then pushed the door open and disappeared inside.

Well, she wasn't very friendly! I turned around to see Pete and Alice bent double, laughing their heads off.

GREAT! HOW AM I GOING TO LIVE THIS ONE DOWN?!

Once Alice and Pete had finally stopped cracking up – honestly, I still don't think it was *that* funny – we made our way inside. A burly security guard escorted us to the canteen to wait until the producer's PA came to get us. After the embarrassing incident with Wendy, I was determined to be on my best behaviour and show everyone I was totally cool about hanging out behind the scenes on the biggest soap in the country. Just then, we walked past a familiar-looking man and, without thinking, I automatically said, 'Hi, Dave.' The man looked at me and rolled his eyes. 'It's Mike, actually.'

Nooooooo! I'd only gone and done it again! What was up with me? The guy played Dave, the hard-nut ex-gangster owner of local restaurant, Amigos, in *Honeydale*. The actor's real name, as he'd just pointed out to me, was Mike. I had to get a grip. I was in serious danger of turning into my nan. She'd once stopped a woman in the street and interrogated her for about an hour about where she knew her from: had they gone to the same school? Was she a friend of her friend Anne? Had she seen her at the hairdresser's? No? What about at Trotter's – the local café? It turned out she saw her three times a week on TV in *The Bill*. Talk about embarrassing!

And now I was doing practically the same thing! But honestly, I couldn't help it. It was totally bizarre to see all these characters everywhere and realise they all have lives outside *Honeydale*. It was like seeing Harry Potter walking down Borehurst High Street, or Shrek buying crisps in the corner shop.

Before I could embarrass myself any further, a girl in her twenties rushed over to us. She was short, with cropped hair and glasses, which she kept pushing nervously up her nose.

'Hi, I'm Kathy, I'm the floor manager. You're the guys from *Star Secrets*, right?'

'That's right,' said Pete, standing up. 'I'm Pete and this is . . .'

'Great, that's great,' interrupted the girl, consulting a piece of paper and obviously not listening. 'OK, if you'd like to come with me, Cassie St Claire wants to meet you all personally in her dressing room.'

I nearly passed out! I couldn't believe it. I was actually going to meet Cassie St Claire. In the last year on *Honeydale*, she had quickly captured the nation's heart with her portrayal of tough-on-the-outside, softer-than-ice-cream-on-the-inside shop owner Tricia Kelly, with a love life more complicated than one of Nan's favourite murder mysteries. Alice looked at me and grinned.

'You have the best job *ever*!' I said.

'I know!' she winked back.

We had to walk through the set to get to Cassie St Claire's dressing room, which took ages and ages. It was unbelievable to see that the rooms that appeared on the telly and seemed so real were actually just sets. Each room only had three walls to allow for the cameras. The three of us had to keep stopping and staring.

'Oooh, look, there's Dave's front room!' said Pete.

'Wow, Tricia's bedroom – looks much bigger on TV, doesn't it?' remarked Alice.

'I always thought Amigos was an actual restaurant – I can't believe it's only a set!' I exclaimed. 'It looks so real, doesn't it?'

Every time we stopped, the floor manager tapped her foot and tried to hurry us along. When we paused to admire the wallpaper in the William's family's kitchen, she practically exploded with impatience.

'Will you all just hurry up?' she snapped. We turned and looked at her in surprise. Kathy seemed quite as taken aback as the rest of us at her outburst. She pushed her glasses up her nose and blinked nervously at us all. 'I'm sorry, it's just that Miss St Claire doesn't have all day. She's got scenes to film after the interview and one of them needs to be re-written.'

'Of course,' said Pete. 'Sorry.'

The three of us hurried behind her, trying our best to ignore the rest of the set. Eventually we got to a corridor with an identical row of white doors, except for one halfway down on the right, which was painted pink. Kathy had just raised her hand to knock, when the door was suddenly flung open and a girl ran out, sobbing. Seeing us standing outside, the girl stopped for a moment, looking absolutely appalled, before bursting into even louder floods of tears and running off down the corridor.

Me, Pete and Alice all looked at each other, not quite sure what to do. The floor manager cleared her throat nervously before knocking twice on the now open door and ushering us in.

'Miss St Claire, the journalists from *Star Secrets* are here,' she said.

Cassie St Claire leapt up from her dressing table, flicking back her famous blonde hair. She was dressed in her 'Tricia' clothes – jeans so tight I was surprised she could sit down, heels so high they made me dizzy just looking at them and a top that was about the size of one of Nan's hankies.

'I'm so glad to meet you all,' she smiled. Her voice was all twinkly and melodious, completely different from the Liverpool accent Tricia spoke with on *Honeydale*. 'Please do come in,' she added.

As we stepped inside, I gave myself a quick talking-to – I'd made enough of an idiot of myself already today. And I really, *really* wanted to make a good impression on Cassie St Claire.

I couldn't help but gawp at her dressing room. It was like something you'd see on a movie.

Seriously. *Everything* was white – the carpet, the walls, the sofa, even the picture frames. And on every available surface there were vases filled with white flowers. I thanked my lucky stars I didn't suffer from hay fever.

'And Kathy?' Cassie addressed the floor manager. 'How many times do I have to tell you, please don't call me Miss St Claire. You know we don't stand on ceremony here.'

Maybe it was just the reflection of all that white on her face, but I could have sworn Kathy turned pale. 'Yes, Miss St – I mean, Cassie,' she said, pushing her glasses up her nose for the zillionth time.

Cassie St Claire turned to us. 'I'm so sorry, you've caught me unawares. The girl you saw a minute ago had just received some bad news from home. The poor thing, I was trying to comfort her – she's terribly upset. We're just one big happy family here. Trouble for one of us affects us all.'

'I'm sorry to hear that,' said Pete. 'If this is a bad time, we could come back later.'

'No, no, I wouldn't hear of it,' smiled Cassie. 'Do sit down and we can all have a nice cosy chat before we start the interview.' She gestured to the big white sofa. I shuffled across the white carpet, keeping my fingers firmly crossed that the bottoms of my shoes were clean. (I mean, can you imagine the embarrassment if I *had* accidentally trodden in dog poo or something? Abs and Soph would never let me live it down!) As I trekked across the room, I suddenly noticed that a photo frame and vase of flowers lay smashed on the floor. The water from the flowers was seeping into the carpet.

'Oh, dear,' twinkled Cassie St Claire, catching me looking. 'You've caught me in a bit of mess. The studio cat got into my dressing room and, as you can see, he's caused a bit of havoc.' She laughed melodiously. 'Such a dear little thing.'

I paused halfway through lowering myself gingerly on to the sofa and looked at Cassie St Claire in surprise. I knew I had read somewhere very recently that Cassie St Claire was hugely allergic to animals, and as a result none of the residents of *Honeydale* owned a pet. Not even a goldfish.

Hmmm. I could definitely feel my mystery radar kicking into gear.

Chapter Four

After about twenty minutes of chitchat with Cassie St Claire, me and Alice left Peter to get on with the interview. Kathy took us back on to the set so we could start getting the info we needed about what a day on *Honeydale* was like. Alice went over to speak to one of the producers, to run through where she was allowed to go and who she could interview. Me and Kathy stood in the corridor by a window, out of everyone's way. I glanced over at Kathy, who was staring stonily ahead.

'I'm so excited to be here,' I said.

'Good,' she answered, without looking at me.

'I'm only on work experience,' I said. 'So I really can't believe I'm on the set of *Honeydale*.'

'Right,' she said.

We stood in a très uncomfortable silence for a little bit longer. I stared out of the window, searching for inspiration. 'Um, nice weather, isn't it?' I said.

Kathy looked at me as if I'd said the most daft thing in the world. She wasn't to know that I *always* say the first thing that pops into my head. Seriously, it's like a disease. She shrugged and walked away. I stared after her. What was with her? Honestly, I was only trying to be friendly. I became aware of someone waving, trying to get my attention.

It was Mike – the actor I'd made an idiot of myself in front of earlier in the canteen. I walked over to him. He was sitting, his head in his hands, with a script in front of him.

'Don't mind Kathy,' he said. 'She doesn't mean

to be horrible. She takes her job very seriously and she just gets a bit stressed sometimes trying to keep everyone happy.' He looked down at his hands. 'We all do,' he added, under his breath.

I could kind of understand that. If I worked on *Honeydale*, I'd take my job pretty seriously too. I glanced over at Kathy, who was now talking into her mobile over on the other side of the set. As I watched, she ran her hand over her face and shook her head, obviously stressed out by whatever the person on the other end of the phone was saying. I made up my mind to be extra nice the next time I spoke to her.

'You know,' said Mike, 'you calling me Dave this morning really got me thinking.'

'Er, I'm so sorry about that,' I cringed. 'I really don't know what came over me. Of course, I know you're not really Dave – I think it was just the excitement of being on set.'

'You're not the first person to do it,' he sighed. 'It happens all the time. Only the other day, an old lady bashed me over the head with her umbrella in the supermarket cos she said I should be ashamed of the way I'd treated Maddie. She told me I needed to stop solving everything with fisticuffs and get myself some help. I tried to explain it wasn't real, that I'm just a character in a soap, but she wasn't having any of it.'

'Really?' I said. 'That's terrible.'

'I mean, I'm a person. I have feelings too. I'm not this hard man that everyone thinks I am. I like poetry. I like kittens.'

'Right,' I nodded. 'Of course you do.'

'In fact,' he said, standing up decisively, 'I'm going to talk to one of the producers now. I'm going to demand we start seeing a softer side to Dave. Maybe he could start hosting poetry nights in the restaurant, or he could save a puppy from drowning in the local park. Yes, I really think I'm on to something here. Thanks a lot,' he smiled and patted me on the shoulder, 'You've been a big help.' And he strode off towards the producers' office.

WHAT THE CRUSTY OLD GRANDADS!

MIKE WAS CERTAINLY NOTHING LIKE DAVE!

I walked over to Alice, who was talking to the members of the camera crew, asking them what time they had to be on set, how long was an average day, how many times did they usually have to shoot scenes, how many cameras were used at any one time and so on, holding her dictaphone up and occasionally scribbling notes into her notepad.

'Hi,' she smiled at me. 'Do you think you're up to doing an interview with some of the crew yourself?'

'Me? Really?' I said. 'Um, I mean, definitely. I'd love to. Actually, Alice, one of the make-up girls is a friend of a friend, so maybe I could find her and ask her what being a make-up artist on *Honeydale* is like?'

'Great idea,' nodded Alice, searching through her bag and pulling out a pile of stuff. 'OK, I've got a list of questions for you here – just the normal stuff, like what time do you start work, how long do people spend in make-up, how do you decide what a character's look should be like, all that sort of thing. Here's a dictaphone for you and a notepad. It's a good idea to scribble down as many details as you can, like what the make-up girl is wearing, what she looks like, how much make-up *she* wears, what the room is like – that makes the feature really come alive and the reader feels almost like they're there themselves.'

'OK, will do.' I was practically exploding with excitement. My first ever interview!!! Sacré bleu! Wait till everyone heard about this. Amanda Witchface Dork-Hawkins would die of jealousy. And, believe me, it couldn't happen to a nicer person!

'Kathy?' Alice called the floor manager, who came striding over, pushing her glasses up her nose. 'Would you mind showing Rosie where the make-up room is? She's going to do an interview.'

'Sure,' said Kathy, nodding at me. 'Please come this way.'

I followed her down yet another corridor.

Honestly, the place was like a rabbit warren! The walls were covered with signed pictures of past and present stars of *Honeydale*. My head swivelled about as we walked. I suddenly remembered the promise I'd made to myself to be extra-friendly to Kathy.

'Wow!' I said, 'Kathy, you're so lucky! It must be amazing to work here every day.'

'Hmm,' she said.

'I mean, to see all these famous people,' I gestured at the framed photos on the walls, 'every single day. To work with them all. You're so lucky!'

'Hmmmm,' said Kathy, pushing her glasses up her nose.

GREAT. IF WE CAN JUST KEEP UP THIS FASCINATING LEVEL OF CONVERSATION, WE'LL BE BEST FRIENDS IN NO TIME!

Just then, a door right in front of us swung open and two women walked out, their arms linked.

'I've never seen anything like it, and I've worked on loads of different soaps,' said one. 'I mean it's like, step right up, get your humiliation here.'

'Yeah, come and be insulted in front of the rest of the cast and crew,' said the other. 'Work on *Honeydale* and be made to feel like dog poo.'

'Apart from today and tomorrow, mind. All of a sudden she's acting like the nicest person in the world and we're all meant to go along with it, just cos there's journa–'

Kathy cleared her throat loudly. One of the women glanced back over her shoulder and, as she spotted the dictaphone in my hand, her face froze in horror. She nudged her companion.

'Hi. You're from *Star Secrets*, aren't you?' she laughed, nervously. 'Don't pay any attention to us – we're extras and we were just, um, er . . .'

'We were just practising our lines,' said her friend, smiling wildly at me.

'Yes, that's right,' the first woman nodded, 'Practising our lines. Lovely to meet you. Excuse us . . .' And the pair of them practically ran down the corridor, heads close together, whispering frantically and shooting desperate looks back at me over their shoulders.

Hmmm, if they were practising their lines, then I was just about to marry Prince William – and we all know *that*'s never gonna happen. Well, not any time soon anyway. I mean, I'd have to actually meet the guy first. Not to mention, he's England's future king. It was unlikely, put it that way.

'What was all that about?' I asked Kathy.

'No idea,' she said, refusing to look at me. 'Actors are a law unto themselves. Um, make-up is the second door on the left.' She pointed down the corridor. 'If you'll excuse me, I've got some stuff to do.' And pushing her glasses up her nose, she sped off after the extras. For one second, I was tempted to follow her and ask her what was going on. Something was very definitely up. Something that, if I wasn't mistaken, everyone was trying very hard to hide from *Star Secrets* magazine. But I knew Alice was counting on me to do this interview and no way was I going to let her down. Investigating would have to wait – I had a job to do!

Taking a deep breath, I raised my hand to knock on the door, when I suddenly heard noisy sobbing coming from inside. I hesitated for a moment, not sure whether I should knock on the door and let whoever was inside know someone was there, or whether I should walk away and come back in a little while. While I was trying to decide, I couldn't help but overhear the conversation inside. It was something like this:

First voice: Sniff . . . *I can't . . . take* . . . sob . . . *much* . . . sniff . . . *more of this. I mean, this morning* . . . sniff . . . *she told me that the flowers were the* . . . sob . . . *wrong shade of white* . . . sob . . .

Second voice: *(angrily) The wrong shade of white? How many shades of white are there? That's the most ridiculous thing I've ever heard!*

First voice: Sob . . . *I know . . . and* . . . sniff . . . *she said that the* . . . sob . . . *fruit salad wasn't sliced to the* . . . sob . . . *right size and* . . . sniff . . . *that the temperature in the room was* . . . sob . . . *two degrees too low* . . . sob . . .

Second voice: *That's just stupid!*
First voice: Sniff . . . *I know . . . but*
. . . sob . . . *she says* . . . sob . . . *if I don't*
get everything right . . . sniff . . . *tomorrow,*
then I'll be out on my ear . . . sob . . . *and*
she'll . . . sob . . . *make sure I don't ever*
work in this business again . . . sob . . .
sob . . . howl! . . .
Second voice: Comforting 'there,
there' noises.

OK, OK, so I knew I sooo shouldn't be
eavesdropping on this conversation. Believe me,
normally I'd have walked away, but I had an
interview to do. Taking a deep breath, I knocked
loudly on the door. Instantly there was silence,
followed by panicked whispering. I knocked again.
There was frantic whispering again, then the door
opened a crack.

'Can I help you?' Two chocolate-brown eyes
peered out at me suspiciously.

'Um, hi. I'm Rosie Parker from *Star Secrets*

magazine. I've come to do an interview with Sally McDonald.'

The woman opened the door wider. I couldn't help but notice she looked a teeny bit relieved.

'Hi, Rosie, I'm Sally,' she said. 'I've heard lots about you from Penny. Come on in.'

Behind her stood the same girl who had run out of Cassie St Claire's dressing room earlier. Mascara had run down her cheeks, her lipstick was smeared and her short pixie hair was standing up on end.

'Um, this is Helen, Cassie St Claire's PA,' said Sally.

The girl gave me a wobbly smile before giving Sally a really big hug.

'Thanks, Sal, you've been great,' she said. 'I'll see you later. Nice to meet you, Rosie,' she said, and quickly scooping up her bag, she left the room.

'Sorry about that,' smiled Sally, pulling her long, blonde hair into a pony tail. 'Make yourself comfy,' she said, gesturing to a big black chair in front of a mirror. She plonked herself down on another chair opposite mine. Although she was friendly, I could tell she wasn't at ease. Her smile never quite reached her eyes. I couldn't help feeling a little bit disappointed that she was so obviously uncomfortable around me – after all, this was one of Penny's best friends. I was determined to get her to relax.

'Are you ready to start the interview, Sally? I asked.

'I have to admit, I've never talked to a journalist before, so I'm not quite sure what to expect,' said Sally, nervously fiddling with the hem of her dress. I checked the dictaphone was working, then placed it on the shelf between us.

'Don't tell anyone, but I've never done an interview before either,' I grinned back at her, 'And I'm not really a journalist.' I waved the list of questions Alice had given me. 'Look, I've even been told what to ask you. I'm only on work experience, you see.'

I waggled my eyebrows at her and the two of us giggled conspiratorially together. Pretty soon,

Sally was happily answering all my questions. Both of us forgot about the dictaphone and it was like having a chat with an old friend. I was even coming up with my own questions!

'So, is being a make-up artist on a soap as glam as it sounds?' I asked.

Sally laughed and shook her head. 'Try having to get out of bed at three-thirty in the morning, so you can make sure all the cast that have early starts are made up and ready to go,' she said. 'Especially when you've had to work late the night before. Just see how glam you feel then.'

Sacré bleu! I didn't even know that time of morning existed! Sally laughed at the look of horror on my face.

'It's worth it, though,' she said with a wink. 'If you can make it through six months of working on *Honeydale*, then you can get a job pretty much anywhere. Even Hollywood. That's what I tell myself, anyway, when it all gets too much,' she added, practically under her breath, suddenly looking more serious.

'So, are the early starts and late nights the worst thing about working on a soap?' I asked.

Sally sighed and looked down at her shoes. 'Try cast members with egos the size of planets who think the world revolves around them –'

'Ahem!' Someone cleared their throat loudly and we both jumped. Sally's hand flew to her mouth as she realised that Cassie St Claire had crept into the room and was standing behind her.

'Ha, ha . . .' Sally let out a laugh that sounded as false as the eyelashes she had in her make-up kit. 'Of course, Rosie, that last bit was just a joke. Ha ha!' She grinned wildly at Cassie St Claire. 'I want to make it clear that every single cast member on *Honeydale* is a pleasure to work with.'

'Oh, Sally.' Cassie's voice was like treacle. She smiled at the pair of us, but I could see her eyes were like stone. 'You and your little jokes! I heard you were doing an interview. Don't let me interrupt, I can see you're busy. But do you think you could pop along and see me later? I need a word.'

'O-o-of course, Miss St Claire,' stammered Sally. 'As soon as I've finished here.'

Cassie St Claire smiled at us both again, then shut the door behind her.

Sally stared at the closed door for a few seconds, an unreadable expression on her face, before smiling rather shakily at me. 'Um, that bit about the cast members really was a joke, Rosie.' She leant towards the dictaphone and spoke directly into it. 'Everyone at *Honeydale* really is a complete pleasure to work with. I mean, *everyone*.'

Even blindfold I would have known she was lying. Something was definitely up, and I was determined to find out what!

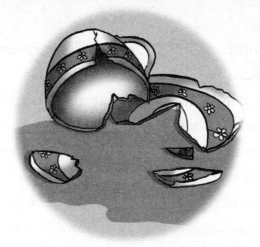

Chapter Five

I spent the rest of the day on set with Alice, getting as much background info as we could. Pete had finished his interview with Cassie St Claire and was busy interviewing other key cast members. I talked to lots of different people, like Simon. He was the props guy. His job was to buy or make every single thing that was used on set, like the menus in Amigos and the pegs Mrs Lynn used to hang up her washing. I even spoke to Mrs Maynard, who ran the canteen. The more people I talked to, the more I heard the same line over and over again. 'If you can last six months on *Honeydale*, you can make it anywhere.' Actually, when I thought about it, no one I'd spoken to on set had worked there for longer than six months. My mystery radar was kicking into megadrive, let me tell you.

I couldn't help comparing the atmosphere on set to the mood in the *Star Secrets* office the previous day. That had buzzed more than a hive of bees having a party. It just felt like everyone genuinely cared about each other. Like when Suze, the editorial assistant, had rounded the corner out of the kitchen at high speed and bumped smack bang into Belle coming the other way. The two had collided with such force that Suze had spilt coffee all down Belle's pale cream smock top.

'I'm so sorry,' Suze had gasped.

'Don't worry,' Belle had winked. 'I'll pretend it's a fashion statement.'

A very similar thing had happened on *Honeydale* earlier that afternoon. Helen had fetched a cup of coffee for one of the producers and was on her way back with it. She totally failed to spot the length of cable in front of her, or the fact that her left foot was heading straight for it. The coffee went flying through the air, splashing at the feet of Cassie St Claire. The teeny-tiniest-so-small-you-could-hardly-see-it drop of coffee speckled her jeans, but from the fuss she made you'd have thought Helen had walked up and thrown a bucket of the stuff all over her deliberately. I'm not joking.

Now, I may not be a maths genius – just ask my teacher, Mr Adams! – but, putting the coffee incident together with the stuff I'd overheard the extras saying, plus the conversation Helen and Sally had been having before I knocked on the door, and it all added up to something decidedly fishier than a tuna sandwich. And one thing I knew for sure was that the mood on set *definitely* had something to do with Cassie St Claire.

I tried asking a few people about what she was like to work with, but over and over again I got the same answer that Sally had given me after Cassie had come into the room. Honestly, if I heard 'everyone on *Honeydale* is a complete pleasure to work with' one more time I was going to scream. Seriously, it was like interviewing a bunch of robots! And surely it couldn't be a coincidence that any time me or Alice were interviewing anyone, Cassie would always appear just to 'check everything's OK'. Check what people were saying, more like!

There was only one thing for it – I was going to have to get someone to open up to me and tell me what was really going on. But short of issuing everyone with a questionnaire about working with Cassie St Claire, I didn't know what to do.

Oooh, now hang on a minute! Hmmm, a questionnaire. Maybe that's not such a bad idea . . .

Questionnaire about working with Cassie St Claire:

Name:
Age:
Job:

1. How would you describe your working relationship with Cassie St Claire?

a) V. nice

b) I don't like her

c) She's a complete witch-troll and makes my life totally miserable

d) Don't know

2. In general, would you prefer not to work with women whose names begin with:

a) C

b) D

c) R

d) Don't know

3. Have you ever wished any particular *Honeydale* character could be killed off?

a) No, they're all lovely

b) Yes, she manages a shop

c) That's the scriptwriters' job. I couldn't possibly get involved

d) Don't know

But if no one was opening up to me when I was interviewing them, they were hardly likely to fill in a questionnaire on the subject, were they?!

I was distracted by a loud crash. Helen had been getting more and more clumsy as the day went on. So far, there'd been the coffee incident, then she'd spilt a glass of water all over Mike's script and made a ladder topple over, nearly hitting one of the camera guys on the head.

Now she was standing in front of Cassie St Claire, who was sitting in a director's chair, a bone china cup and saucer lying smashed at her feet. What was it with all these dropped drinks?

'I'm s-s-so sorry,' Helen was stammering. 'I don't kn-kn-know what happened. I . . . it just slipped out of my hands.'

Cassie leapt up, an angry frown flashing across her face. A look of pure terror swept across Helen's.

'You stu–' Cassie began saying, then paused as she noticed Alice, who had looked up from interviewing one of the producers to see what all the commotion about.

Cassie St Claire laughed a tinkly laugh. 'You silly thing,' she smiled. 'I never liked that cup and saucer anyway.' She raised her eyebrows at Alice. 'You know, I've never understood why I'm not just given a normal mug, like everyone else.'

A slight frown furrowed Alice's brow before she shrugged and turned back to continue her interview.

Cassie St Claire carried on laughing her tinkly laugh. 'Helen, dear, maybe you should go and work in the office,' she said. 'Before you have any more little accidents.' Helen winced, then scuttled from the room, knocking a chair flying in her rush. She looked terrified.

Cassie turned to the rest of us and smiled, but not before I'd seen her flick a look of complete and utter disgust at her PA. 'I know,' she beamed at no one in particular, 'why don't I go and get tea for everyone?'

I decided to try and catch up with Helen to make sure she was OK. As I walked across the set, I passed two of the cameramen who were muttering together. 'I'm surprised she even knows where the canteen is – it's not like she ever eats with us. She has all her meals specially delivered to her dressing room.'

'Yeah, and the day she drinks from a mug like the rest of us is the day I come to work starkers. And believe me, mate, that's never gonna –' he broke off as he saw me approaching. 'Er, like I was saying, everyone on *Honeydale* is a complete pleasure to work with.'

* * *

I managed to catch up with Helen in the corridor.

'Are you all right?' I asked.

'Yes, fine,' she shrugged, refusing to look at me.

'Oh, good. It's just, you seemed a little upset back there.'

'Not at all,' she said.

'Well, you know where I am if you want a chat,' I said, tailing off lamely as, surprise, surprise, Cassie clip-clopped up the corridor behind us. *Honestly, does the woman have a built-in radar system or something?*

'Everything all right here?' she asked.

Helen froze in horror.

'Yes, fine,' I said quickly. 'Helen was just telling me what a pleasure everyone at *Honeydale* is to work with.'

Helen smiled at me gratefully before hurrying off down the corridor.

Cassie watched her go. 'Such a dear little thing,' she said to me. 'She's had bad news from home, you know.'

Yeah, right. After a day at *Honeydale*, one thing I knew for sure was that Cassie St Claire was as fake as the set itself.

Chapter Six

Later that night, me and Penny were sitting at her kitchen table, eating fish and chips straight out of the paper. We were meant to have been having shepherd's pie, but when we sat down to eat it, the mashed potato was burnt, while the meat was still totally raw. I mean, like, properly eww! Cooking is sooo not Penny's thing.

I was happily digging out those last few chips from the bottom of the bag. You know, the ones which are, like, completely crispy and totally yumsville. I was noisily licking the vinegar off my fingers when the doorbell rang. Penny got up to answer it. She came back in a few minutes later with Sally, who looked really upset. I pushed the rest of my chips away and stood up.

'What's going on?' I asked.

Penny shook her head at me and put her finger to her lips before putting the kettle on. Sally sank into one of the kitchen chairs and burst into noisy sobs – proper, big, shoulder-heaving sobs which she had no control over. Penny rushed over and hugged her, while I grabbed a box of tissues and passed them to her. Sally blew her nose loudly and took a deep, shuddery breath.

'I-can't-*sniff*-believe-it-*sob*-Cassie's-had-me-sacked,' she sobbed.

Penny rubbed her back. 'I can't understand you, honey,' she said soothingly. 'Slow down and tell us what's going on.'

Sally blew her nose again.

'Cassie St Claire's had me sacked,' she hiccupped.

'WHAT?!!!' me and Penny both said at once.

Sally took a deep breath. 'Cassie heard me talking to Rosie earlier. I said that the worst part of the job was working with cast members that had egos the size of planets. And even though I said it was a joke, Cassie went to the producers and told them I'd been slandering her to a journalist, and either they sacked me or she'd walk. And the producers called me in and said that they were sorry but, seeing as Cassie St Claire was the biggest thing to happen to *Honeydale* since Sandra Matthews had an affair with her sister's husband, they had no choice but to let me go. And Cassie stood there behind them smirking while they were saying all this. And then she said that she knows everyone in the industry, so if I think I can just walk into another job, I've got another think coming.'

Sally started sobbing helplessly again, leaning on Penny for support and dripping big wet tears on to her chest.

I sank into one of the kitchen chairs, tears filling my eyes. This was all my fault. I felt terrible. 'Sally, I'm so sorry. If I hadn't been interviewing you, you'd have never said that, and Cassie would never have heard you – and you'd never have been sacked. I'm so sorry.'

'Don't worry, Rosie,' said Penny. 'None of this is your fault.'

'She's-right-you-know-it's-not-your-fault-it's-Cassie-she's-a-big-fat-bully,' sobbed Sally.

'Er, sorry, I didn't quite catch that,' I said.

Sally let out another big hiccup. 'Penny's right, it's not your fault, Rosie,' she said, reaching out to take my hand. 'Cassie St Claire's just a big fat bully. But because she's a big star and has, like, tripled *Honeydale's* ratings, no one can say anything.'

The kettle had boiled and Penny got up to make tea, getting a lemonade out of the fridge for me.

'Tell us everything from the beginning, Sal,' she said, pushing a steaming mug of tea in front of her.

Sally took a big slurp.

'Basically, Cassie's been a complete witch since

she started on *Honeydale* six months ago. But since the ratings have soared and she won all those soap awards, her behaviour's got out of control. Everyone's too scared to do anything, though.

'She told Helen today that because she hadn't got her the same amount of coverage in *TV Central* mag as Alison Stiner, who plays Lara Shallcross in *Honeydale*'s rival soap, *The Village*, she was the worst PA she'd ever had. And that the reason she was the worst PA she'd ever had and is so bad at her job, is because Helen isn't a likeable person. And then she told her she'd put on weight. She's just a horrible, horrible woman.'

Penny and me stared at each other, totally horrified, while Sally took another big slug of her tea, before carrying on.

'She once rang me up at midnight to tell me that she'd just watched an episode and I'd used the wrong shade of eyeshadow on her. She had me on the phone for over an hour, screaming and shouting at me and saying that I'd ruined the whole episode because it just wasn't the sort of eyeshadow her character would wear. I wouldn't mind, but she specifically requested that particular shade herself.

'She treats everyone the same way – she's even thrown things at people. She's made practically every single person who works on *Honeydale* cry. And you know what the worst thing is? Whenever she shouted at anyone else in front of me, instead of stepping in, I would just sit there thanking my lucky stars it wasn't me she was having a go at.

'The only thing that kept me going was the hope that tomorrow would be better. But it never was.

'When she heard you lot from *Star Secrets* were coming in, she obviously had a huge panic that you'd find out what she's really like. So she made the producers send an email round. It said that anyone caught saying anything other than that every cast member of *Honeydale* was a complete pleasure to work with, would be severely reprimanded.

'And now she's gone and had me sacked and I'll

probably never get another job . . .' Sally burst into floods of tears again.

'But there must be *something* you can do?' I said, horrified. 'I mean, can't you go to her boss – the producers or something – and tell them what she's like?'

'No one can do a thing,' Sally said, shaking her head miserably. 'Whenever Cassie doesn't get her own way, she threatens to go and get a job on a rival soap, so the bosses always end up caving in. The producers know they can always get another cameraman, or another PA, or even another make-up artist, but they can't get another Cassie St Claire.'

'Don't worry, Sal,' said Penny, 'We'll think of something. Honestly.'

'Too right we will,' I said firmly. I only wished I felt as confident as I sounded.

* * *

I instant-messaged Abs and Soph a bit later, having left Penny and Sally talking in the kitchen:

NosyParker: Who'd have thought Cassie St Claire was such a witch?

FashionPolice: That's even worse than stonewashed jeans with a stonewashed jacket.

(Let me just say that that, coming from Soph, is seriously bad indeed . . .)

CutiePie: So, what's Sally going to do?

NosyParker: That's the thing, Abs. She doesn't think there's anything she can do. Except try and get another job.

CutiePie: I hate to say it, but she's probably right – especially if her bosses already know what Cassie St Claire's like. You could try talking to them, but I don't fancy your chances.

That was worrying. If Abs, who basically has a brain the size of a planet – seriously, she's the smartest person I know – didn't think there was anything that could be done, then there probably wasn't much I *could* do. I signed off and decided to ring home.

Nan answered the phone with an annoyed, 'Hello!'

'It's me, Nan. I thought I'd ring for a chat.'

'A *chat*?'

'Yes! What's wrong with that?'

'Well, *Midsomer Murders* is on. Everyone knows that. No one rings at this time. Ever.'

WHATEVER HAPPENED TO GRAND-MOTHERS WHO WERE OVER THE MOON TO HEAR FROM THEIR ONLY GRAND-DAUGHTER, THAT'S WHAT I WANT TO KNOW?!

'Oh. Right, sorry. I forgot, Nan. I'll ring back later.'

'No, it's OK – I've seen this one before anyway.'

HONESTLY!

I filled Nan in on the day's events quickly, before she could get distracted by her favourite actor, John Nettles, solving yet another case in what must be the most murder-ridden village ever! I mean, I don't know if you've ever seen it, but it's all set in a place called Midsomer, and in every single episode about three people are bumped off. Seriously. I mean, no one in their right mind would ever move there – you must have something like a nine-out-of-ten chance of meeting a grisly death. Surely estate agents would have to warn you before you bought a house in the area!

Anyway, Nan listened to the whole story. Then she said, 'Well, Rosie, it all seems very simple to me.'

'Really?'

'Yes, it's just like that made-for-TV film we watched the night before you went to London. You know, the one where they exposed the bully at the end. That's all you have to do.'

'What? You mean I should tie Cassie St Claire to a chair and hold her at gunpoint until she confesses? Na-a-a-an!' I said, totally outraged, 'You can't be serious! Do you want me to end up in prison?'

'Rosie Parker,' Nan sighed. 'I sometimes

wonder if you really are my granddaughter. Of course that's not what I mean.'

Oh.

'I mean, Rosie,' Nan continued, 'tell everyone what she's really like. That's the one thing bullies can't stand – being shown up for the weak cowards they actually are.'

And like a lightbulb going off in my head, a plan popped into my mind.

'Thanks, Nan,' I grinned down the phone. 'You're a total star.'

Chapter Seven

The next morning, I set off to meet Pete and Alice in a café round the corner from the studio. Pete stood up and gave me a humongous hug the minute I walked in.

'You are a total genius, Miss Parker,' he grinned, 'I couldn't believe it when you rang me last night. Sit down. I've already ordered fry-ups all round, so I hope you're hungry. Got to keep your strength up for the day ahead.'

Two minutes later, the bell over the door dinged as Alice walked into the café. 'What's going on?' she asked. 'How come we're meeting here? I thought we were going straight to the studio this morning.'

Pete winked at me. 'Slight change of plan. I'll let Rosie fill you in.'

I paused for a mo while the café owner brought over three scrumissimo plates piled sky-high with sausages, bacon, beans, tomatoes, mushrooms, eggs and toast. Then I started to tell Alice the events of the night before, up to the phone conversation with Nan.

'Your nan sounds a riot,' said Pete, scooping runny egg yolk up with a piece of toast.

'She certainly has her moments,' I said, 'put it that way.'

'But I still don't understand why we're all here,' said Alice.

'Well,' I said, 'after I spoke to Nan, I had a bit of an idea. We need to expose what's really going on and let the whole world know what Cassie St Claire is like.'

'Totally!' said Alice, nodding eagerly. 'But I don't see how we can, unless we get Sally to give us an interview all about what life is *really* like on *Honeydale*.'

'Which she'd never do, cos Cassie St Claire has enough clout in the industry to make sure Sally would never work again,' said Pete.

'Exactly,' I said. 'Which is where we come in. The only way to do it is to get everyone to speak to us as journalists, knowing it's going to be printed in *Star Secrets* magazine . . .'

'On the record . . .' nodded Pete.

'Yep, on the record,' I agreed as if I used journalistic terms like that all the time – *oooh, if Abs and Soph could hear me now* – 'about what Cassie St Claire is really like. But to do that we need everyone to trust us – which is where Sally comes in. She's agreed to pretend to be the photographer's assistant today, which means she'll be able to talk to the cast and crew without Cassie getting suspicious.'

Alice held her hand up. 'Er, sorry, Rosie. Of course Cassie's going to get suspicious when Sally McDonald turns up as the photographer's assistant on a *Star Secrets* shoot and starts interviewing all the cast and crew members. I mean, I met Sally McDonald yesterday and she's pretty recognisable.'

'Ah, but this is the cunning bit,' grinned Pete, pushing his plate away. 'Carry on, Rosie.'

'Don't forget, Sally's a make-up artist, and Penny – who I'm staying with – is a stylist,' I grinned at Alice. 'Between the two of them, they can work some serious magic. I'm not kidding. Even better, the photographer is an old boyfriend of Penny's and the two are still pretty friendly, so he's totally in on the plan and totally up for it!'

'And I spoke to Candy after Rosie rang me last night,' added Pete. 'She thinks it's a great idea, although obviously we're going to have to run the feature past the *Star Secrets* lawyers. She thinks it might be one of the mag's biggest exclusives yet!'

Alice shook her head. 'Sorry, but I still can't see how a bit of make-up and different clothes are going to fool anyone.'

My phone beeped. I quickly checked the

message. I grinned at Alice. 'Hang on a minute.' I went to the café door and opened it.

A girl with short, dark hair and piercing green eyes walked in, dressed in combat trousers, sneakers and a T-shirt.

'Hi, Rosie,' she smiled at me.

'Hi, Ashley,' I grinned. 'Come and sit down.'

We walked over the table and Pete stood up. 'Ah, Ashley Francis, I presume. Rosie's told me a lot about you.'

Alice raised an eyebrow as Ashley pulled up a chair. 'I don't mean to be rude,' she said to the newcomer. 'But we're kind of in the middle of a conversation.'

'Don't mind me,' said Ashley. 'I know all about it.'

'Oh. Right,' said Alice, looking a bit taken aback. 'Well, as I was saying, Rosie, I just don't see how we're going to get away with it. I mean, a bit of make-up isn't going to fool anyone.'

Pete, Ashley and me all burst out laughing. Alice stared at us all, looking completely put out.

'I don't see what's so funny,' she complained. 'This is serious.'

'Well, "a bit of make-up" certainly fooled you,' laughed Pete, grinning at me and Ashley. Alice looked at the three of us like we'd totally lost our minds.

Ashley leant forward. 'Alice,' she said. 'I *am* Sally.'

Alice's jaw fell so far, I was worried it might hit the table! I'm not joking. 'Wh . . . wh . . . what?' she said. 'H-how? But you don't look anything like you.'

Ashley grinned. 'A wig, coloured contact lenses, a bucket-load of make-up and a whole new wardrobe courtesy of Penny – and ta-dah! A whole new person!'

Alice stared at her, completely gob-smacked. Then she slumped back in her chair and gazed at me.

'Rosie,' she said, 'I take it all back. You, girl, are a total genius!' She grinned at me, and jumping up, ran round the table to give me a huge hug.

'What are you waiting for?' she shouted at the others. 'Let's go get ourselves a story!'

* * *

Once we were on the set, me, Alice and Pete set up shop in one of the smaller dressing rooms. It wasn't a patch on Cassie St Claire's – just an old sofa, an old carpet with so many swirls it made me dizzy just looking at it, and a mirror with a big old crack in it. Ben, the photographer and Ashley were out on set, so Ben could take pictures of people as they worked. That meant, as Pete explained to me, the feature would have a real behind-the-scenes feel – much better than lots of posed photographs. Ashley took the opportunity to fill in everyone on how we wanted the feature to become an exposé on Cassie St Claire, so that the world would know what a bully she was and she would no longer be able to get away with her behaviour. And pretty soon people were knocking on the door, wanting to know when they could talk to us.

We were in the middle of interviewing Helen about Cassie's treatment of her. I'd already had to put a new tape into the dictaphone.

'She refused to leave her dressing room until her bowl of sweets arrived,' Helen was saying. 'But not any old bowl of sweets. Oh, no. The bowl could only have red sweets in it. It took me the best part of an hour just to find that many red sweets. When I gave it to her, she said the bowl was the wrong size! And when I tried to apologise, she threw the sweets at me and one hit me in the eye. And she just laughed and said she hoped I got a black eye cos at least it would stop people from noticing how awful my clothes were. Then she said because it had taken me so long to get the sweets, I'd held the whole set up, which cost a lot of money and she was going to make sure it got taken out of my salary.'

'But why didn't you just leave if it was so bad?' Alice asked gently.

'I wanted to,' said Helen, tears filling her eyes. 'But she told me she wouldn't give me a reference and she'd make sure everyone knew what a terrible PA I was and no one would ever employ me. I believed her.'

Alice, Pete and I exchanged glances. It was the same story we'd heard all morning.

'Thanks for sharing your story with us, Helen,' Peter smiled at her. 'Because of you, and everyone who's being brave enough to talk to us today, Cassie St Claire will never be able to bully anyone again.'

'I hope so,' said Helen, tears pouring down her face. 'I really do.'

As she got up, there was a knock on the door.

'Oh, that'll be Mike,' I said. 'He wants to tell us about the time that Cassie made him cry.'

'Really?' said Pete, shaking his head. 'She even reduced hard-man Dave Edwards – ex-gangster-turned-restaurant-owner – to tears?'

'Come in!' I said. The door opened and we all froze. It was Cassie St Claire. For an instant, she looked shocked to see Helen, who was rooted to the spot with terror, a handkerchief halfway to her nose. Then she stepped into the room, a professional smile on her lips.

'Oh, there you all are – I was wondering where you'd got to. I've seen your photographer and his assistant out on the set, but no sign of the rest of you. And here you all are . . . with Helen.'

'Um, yes,' said Pete quickly. 'We were just having a brief editorial conference about what we needed to do, and Helen here was kind enough to step in and ask if we'd like coffee.' He smiled at Helen. 'I do hope that cold gets better soon.'

'Th-thanks,' said Helen, seriously looking like she might actually faint with gratitude. 'I'll get those coffees for you now.' Without looking at Cassie, she half-ran out of the door.

Cassie's eyes roamed around the room, stopping on the dictaphone that was still running on the coffee table. Pete stood up, stepping forward so his body blocked her view.

'Actually, I was just about to come and find you, Miss St Claire,' he smiled. 'Obviously, you're the star of this feature and I'd really appreciate it if we could talk some more. I'm not sure I got everything I needed yesterday. The readers of *Star Secrets* are desperate to know what Cassie St Claire is really like.' He turned back to me and Alice, 'I'll leave you two to get on with the rest of the stuff we discussed.' He smiled at Cassie conspiratorially and said, 'The less important stuff, obviously.'

The tips of Cassie's ears were tinged pink with glee. 'Of course,' she tinkled. 'It'd be my pleasure. Why don't you come to my dressing room?'

As he closed the door behind them, Pete gave us a wink and thumbs-up.

'Phew!' Alice flopped back in her chair. 'That was close! OK, who's next?'

* * *

Five hours later, we left the set, completely exhausted, but with everything we needed. Ben and a grinning Ashley had left the studio an hour earlier, having got all the pictures necessary for the feature.

'I'm exhausted,' I yawned as we walked towards the tube station.

'Go home and get some sleep,' said Pete. 'We've got to get this lot written up tomorrow.'

'I don't know if I'll be able to sleep,' I said. 'I keep thinking about all those awful stories we heard today. How can anyone be allowed to get away with such behaviour?'

'I know,' said Pete putting his arm round my shoulders and giving me a quick squeeze. 'But our feature should help put a stop to it. You've done a great job, Rosie. You should be really proud of yourself.'

'Yeah,' grinned Alice. 'We'll make a journalist of you yet!'

Chapter Eight

The next morning, as I made my way over to my desk in the *Star Secrets* office, I have to admit I was feeling more than a tad hard done by. Penny had gone to bed as soon as I'd got in the night before. She'd said she had to get up at the crack of dawn the next day. I'd been pretty disappointed, as I'd really been looking forward to telling her all about the day's events. And, to be honest, I'd been expecting her to make a bit of a fuss of me. After all, the exposé that was meant to help her friend had been my idea.

I slung my bag on to my desk and turned on my computer. The rest of the features desk was completely deserted. Where were Pete and Alice? I spotted them in Belle's office with Candy, deep in conversation. I raised my hand in a wave as Pete glanced over and gave me a half-smile.

'What's going on?' I mouthed. Pete shrugged his shoulders at me, then turned his attention back to Belle and shook his head emphatically at something she was saying. Candy looked up and caught me watching. She said something to Belle, who got up from her seat and lowered the blinds over the door, so I could no longer see in.

Lolly, who was sporting a bright pink fringe today – she obviously changes her hair as often as her clothes – was whispering at Suze's desk. I got up and walked over to them.

'Hi, guys,' I smiled. 'How's it going?'

'Fine,' said Lolly. 'Sorry, Rosie. Can't chat – I've got loads to do.' And she practically ran back to her desk – well, it would have been a run if she hadn't been wearing five-inch silver stiletto boots.

'OK,' I called after her. I smiled at Suze, but she picked up some files on her desk and started shuffling them importantly. 'Um, actually I'm pretty busy too,' she said.

'Oh, OK,' I said. 'Well, don't mind me, I'm just going to –'

'Fine,' she said, shuffling another file.

Well, honestly. I could have been about to say anything, like, 'Don't mind me, I'm just going to set the office on fire,' or 'I'm just going to run around the office totally naked,' or even, 'Hey, I'm just going to throw myself out of the office window BECAUSE NO ONE SEEMS TO BE TALKING TO ME AND I DON'T KNOW WHAT I'VE DONE!'

Feeling totally miserable, I walked back to my desk and opened up the gossip page I'd started earlier in the week. But my heart wasn't in it, especially when I noticed that Lolly was back at Suze's desk and the two of them were whispering and giggling away, casting looks in my direction. Trying (and totally failing) not to mind, I clicked on my email. To my surprise, there was a message from Nan. Which, let me tell you, has *never* happened before. I didn't even know that Nan knew how to use a computer. Whenever I'm doing my homework on mine, she always mutters about me needing a good old-fashioned typewriter. After all, if it's good enough for Jessica Fletcher (star of *Murder, She Wrote* – Nan's favourite murder mystery), it should be more than good enough for me.

To: NosyParker@hotmail.com
From: MurderMostFoul1@hotmail.com
Subject: Writing

Dear Rosie,
I hope you are well. And I hope you managed to solve your own little mystery after our chat the other day. Anyway, I've decided to start writing my own murder mystery (you're not the only Parker who can write, you know). I've attached the breakdown for the first

episode and thought you could show it to the producers at *Honeydale* and suggest it as a new series?
Your loving Nan.
xxx

I clicked to open the attachment.

There's a serious outbreak of crime in the neighbourhood – someone is stealing all the humbugs and butter toffees. The main suspect is Old Peg Leg down the road, because he's had a suspiciously high number of dental appointments. The local retirement home has been thrown into a toffee-shortage crisis. Only Mrs Barker (who may come across as a vague, murder-mystery-mad old lady on the outside, but has a razor-sharp, crime-solving brain that Sherlock Holmes would be jealous of) can save the day.

WHAT THE CRUSTY OLD GRANDADS?!!

I jumped as someone tapped my shoulder. I spun round. Belle was standing behind me with Candy, Peter and Alice hovering behind her.

'I-I-I'm sorry, Belle. I-I-I was just checking my email. I'll get on with the gossip page now,' I stuttered.

'That's not what I wanted to talk to you about, Rosie,' said Belle, who was looking extremely stern to say the least. Nervously, I glanced at Alice and Pete, but both of them were looking at the floor and totally refused to meet my eyes. The whole office fell silent as Belle continued speaking.

'It's come to my attention that it was you who came up with the idea for turning the behind-the-scenes *Honeydale* piece into an exposé on Cassie St Claire's bullying. I'm afraid, Rosie, I have no choice but to tell you that your behaviour was underhand and sneaky and could have landed *Star Secrets* in a whole lot of trouble. Quite frankly, it's exactly the kind of behaviour . . .'

I stared at the floor, as tears started to prick my

eyes. 'I'm really sorry,' I said, desperately trying not to cry. No way was I going to blub in front of the whole office. Not me. No, sir. No way. 'I didn't think,' I said.

Belle held her hand up, 'I haven't finished, Rosie. As I was saying, this is exactly the kind of behaviour that I look for in my staff.'

WHAT?? DID BELLE JUST SAY WHAT I THOUGHT SHE SAID?

Belle broke into a grin. 'And it's the best story that *Star Secrets* has had in years! Well done, Rosie!'

She leant forward and gave me a huge hug, while the whole office burst into applause.

'You should have seen your face!' laughed Pete.

'We've got another surprise for you,' grinned Alice. 'Come in!' she shouted. I looked up as Penny and Sally – dressed as her normal self – staggered into the office holding a humongous homemade chocolate cake between them with 'Well done Rosie,' spelt out in sweets across the top.

'Um,' I looked at Penny, 'did you make the cake?'

'No, Sally did,' she said.

'In that case, everyone dig in!' I grinned. Penny elbowed me, then burst out laughing and enveloped me in a huge hug.

'Right, everyone . . . I think we've definitely earned a celebratory breakfast,' said Belle. 'Let's go.'

'I'm so sorry we were short with you earlier,' said Lolly, linking her arm through mine as we all piled into Frank's Café down the road. 'Belle told us we weren't allowed to give you even the slightest hint of how pleased she was with the job you did yesterday, so we didn't dare talk to you in case we gave it away.'

I grinned at her and looked happily around at all my new friends, who were merrily ordering huge fry-ups. Pete caught me watching and raised his steaming mug of tea in a toast.

'Here's to you, Rosie. The best work-experience girl we've ever had!'

I felt myself blush as red as the bottles of ketchup on the table.

Belle looked at me and winked. 'Right, everyone, you've got half an hour, then it's back to work. Rosie in particular has a lot to do helping Pete and Alice write up the lead story for the next issue of *Star Secrets* – the *Honeydale* story!'

I beamed back at her, too happy to speak.

Chapter Nine

A couple of weeks later, I was back at home in boring old Borehurst. It was Saturday morning and I was *trying* to have a lie-in – trying, but definitely not succeeding in my madhouse of a home. Downstairs I could hear Mum singing at the top of her voice as she did the washing up. Her eighties tribute band, the Banana Splits, had been booked for a fortieth birthday party that night and she was obviously trying to get in some last-minute practice. I love my mother dearly, honestly I do, but sometimes having a mum whose one mission on earth is to bring the music of her all-time favourite band, Banarama, to a more modern audience is seriously annoying. Her singing was obviously winding Nan up too, as she had her DVD of *Murder, She Wrote* on full-blast. Seriously, it was so loud it was like having Angela Lansbury and all the other wrinkly old cast-members in my bedroom, acting out the episode right next to me. You know, sometimes I really can't help wishing my family could be a little bit more – well – normal.

With all that noise, going back to sleep sooo wasn't an option. Sighing loudly, I flopped my legs over the side of the bed and padded barefoot downstairs to the kitchen.

'Morning, darling,' smiled Mum, turning round from doing the washing-up. 'Sleep well?'

'Till about an hour ago,' I muttered pointedly, pouring some cereal into a bowl. But I was talking to thin air. Mum had turned back to the sink and was busy practising her dance routine as she rinsed out the breakfast things. Honestly, watching your mother shimmying from side to side, dressed in baggy dungarees, a neon-pink off-the-shoulder sweat top and bovver boots is enough to put anyone off their breakfast. (Have I mentioned that Mum also likes to dress 'in character' when she practises? Apparently it helps her get in the mood. Well, it certainly makes *me* moody, that's all I can say.) I rolled my eyes and munched my cereal, grumpily.

'Oh, Rosie, honey,' Mum turned round mid-shimmy, 'I almost forgot – there's some post for you on the table. It's under Nan's *Unsolved Crimes* magazine.'

I reached across the table and pulled out a humongous brown envelope with *Star Secrets* printed in big letters across the top. I ripped it open, my hands trembling a bit with all the excitement. A glossy new copy of the magazine slithered upside-down on to the table in front of me, together with an official-looking envelope. I picked it up and opened it. Ooh, la, la! It was a letter from Belle!

Star Secrets Magazine
Third Floor
18 Piccadilly St
London

To my star reporter, Rosie

I hope you're well! I wanted to thank you again for all your hard work during your time with us. I hope you know you would be welcome back at Star Secrets *at any time and I* really *mean that. I've enclosed the latest issue of the mag for you, which includes not only your prize-winning story, but your first ever scoop – what* really *goes on behind-the-scenes at* Honeydale*! I know it's going to be the first of many for you and hope you will remember us when you're a rich and famous journalist.*

I already have some feature ideas that I think you would be perfect to write for us during your school holidays – Candy will be in touch very soon to talk you through them. And we'll pay you, of course!

Thank you again, Rosie, you're one work-experience girl we'll never forget, and I know we will be speaking again soon.

Take care, and don't forget to let me know what you think of the mag!

Much love
Belle
xxx

No way! Not only was I holding a hand-written letter from the editor of *Star Secrets* in my hand, she was offering me work! And paid work at that! I couldn't believe it. Abs and Soph were going to go CRAZISSIMO when I told them! And as for Amanda Hawkins – she'd explode with jealousy. Ever since I'd been back at school, she and her pathetic cronies had been making snide comments about how I must have loads of paper cuts after opening all that post at *Star Secrets,* cos no way would they ever let anyone like me write anything for the magazine. Ha, ha, ha! In your face, Dork-Hawkins!

I turned over the magazine. There was a huge picture of Cassie St Claire on the cover, and in big letters were the words: BEHIND THE SCENES AT *HONEYDALE*, but the *HONEY* was crossed out and HORROR had been scrawled over it. Quickly, I opened the mag itself. There, on the first page, next to Belle's 'Letter From the Editor', was a big picture of me, sitting at my desk, laughing at something Pete was saying. Even in my excitement, I couldn't help noticing it wasn't the most flattering picture. My hair looked more like a bird's nest than ever and I had a bit of something that looked suspiciously like spinach stuck in my teeth. Nice. WAY TO LOOK ATTRACTIVE, ROSIE!

I quickly averted my eyes and scanned through the editor's letter:

Hi guys, and welcome to another packed issue of Star Secrets *magazine*

Boy, have we got a corker for you! You're not going to be able to put it down, believe me! And it's all thanks to Rosie Parker – our Star Secrets *story-competition winner! Thanks to her intrepid journalistic skills, we have* THE *biggest story of the year – what life is really like on* Honeydale. *It's like something out of the soap itself, but it's all true! Let's just say that Cassie St Claire is not all she seems. Turn over the page NOW and get reading. You're not going to believe it!*

Until next week
Belle
xxx

I flicked over the page and there, next to the headline *HORROR ON HONEYDALE,* were the words '*by Rosie Parker*'!

'Sacré bleu!' I shouted with excitement, dropping the magazine.

'What? What?' said Mum, hurrying over and fishing the mag out of my cereal bowl where it had landed. She wiped the milk off it on her dungarees and opened it. She looked at the page in silence for a moment, then screamed with delight and enveloped me in a humongous hug. The two of us danced around the kitchen, laughing and shrieking.

'What on earth is going on?' Nan was standing in the kitchen doorway, staring at us like we'd totally lost our minds. 'Honestly,' she grumbled, 'From all the noise, I thought someone had been murdered!'

'Your granddaughter is a real-life journalist,' beamed Mum, waving *Star Secrets* at Nan.

'You haven't even heard the best bit yet,' I grinned. 'Take a look at this!' I passed her the letter from Belle. Mum read it, then looked at me, her eyes brimming with tears. 'Rosie Parker, I am so proud of you,' she said.

'Thanks, Mum,' I said, embarrassingly close to tears myself.

'This calls for a serious celebration,' said Nan, bustling over to the kitchen cupboards. 'Now where did I put those custard creams?'

'Never let it be said that the Parker family don't know how to party!' Mum said, winking at me.

I left Mum and Nan poring over *Star Secrets* – neatly side-stepping Nan's question about what the *Honeydale* producers had thought of her murder-mystery synopsis – and went upstairs to call Abs and Soph. I was just rooting around in my bag for my mobile when it started ringing. I fished it out.

'Hello?' I said.

'Is that Rosie?' asked a female voice. It was familiar, but I couldn't quite place it.

'Yes,' I said. 'Who's calling?'

'Cassie St Claire,' said the voice.

I nearly dropped the phone with shock.

'Rosie, I know I'm probably the last person you expected – or probably wanted – to hear from,' said Cassie. She could certainly say that again.

'H-h-how did you get my number?' I stammered.

'Your number was on the contact sheet *Star Secrets* faxed over to the production office the first day you came to the set. And I'm very glad it was, especially now I've read your feature.'

I sat down on the bed, shaking. Revealing Cassie St Claire's temper in *Star Secrets* was one thing, but I wasn't sure I could handle being on the receiving end of it.

'Anyway,' Cassie continued. 'I wanted to let you know that as of today, thanks to you and *Star Secrets*, I have officially been sacked from *Honeydale* and your friend Sally has been given her job back. The producers said they had no choice but to get rid of me before *Honeydale*'s ratings started falling. Apparently, I'm an embarrassment and a risk to *Honeydale*'s ratings. You know, Rosie, I've lost everything. My job, my reputation – *everything.*'

I couldn't listen to this any longer. 'You know what, Cassie?' I burst out. 'It's not what I wanted. But, yes, I'm pleased Sally's got her job back, and I'm really happy that people don't have to put up with your behaviour any longer. You deserved to be sacked. You can't get away with treating people like that!'

'Rosie, you don't understand . . .'

'I understand all right,' I interrupted angrily. 'I understand that you are a complete and total bully.'

There was silence at the end of the phone and then a noise that sounded suspiciously like a sniff, followed by a muffled sob. If I hadn't known better, I could have sworn that Cassie St Claire was crying.

'Rosie, you're right,' she said, eventually. 'Your feature made me take a long, hard look at my behaviour. I'm not trying to excuse myself – there are no excuses for the way I've treated people. But I wanted to let you know that I've decided to get help. I'm going to a clinic in America for a month to deal with my anger issues. I know I have a long way to go, and a lot of bridges to mend and I don't know if I'll ever get work as an actress again, but it's a start. So really I was ringing to say thank you. In a strange sort of way, your feature has probably done me a favour.'

'Oh,' I said. 'Right.'

'Thanks, Rosie,' said Cassie in a very quiet voice. 'Thanks for everything. And I really mean that.'

'Good luck, Cassie,' I said. 'And I really mean that.'

I pressed 'end' on my mobile and stared at it, totally gobsmacked. Almost immediately it rang again. I almost jumped out of my skin.

'Hi, Rosie?' said another female voice that I couldn't quite place. Seriously, it was like *Groundhog Day*. 'It's Belle. I just wanted to check you got my package.'

'Belle!' I said. 'You couldn't have chosen a better time to call!'

I quickly filled her in on my conversation with Cassie.

'Rosie, that's amazing!' she said. 'Cassie St Claire ringing to apologise – who'd have guessed.' She paused. 'Actually, I've just had a thought. When she comes out of the clinic, we should do an interview with her. Our readers will be dying to find out what happened after she got sacked.'

'Oooh, definitely!' I said. 'It's just like a real-life soap story.'

'Exactly,' agreed Belle. 'And Rosie, I think you should be the person to write it.'

'Really? Me?'

'Definitely you!' laughed Belle.

I had a lump in my throat. I swallowed a couple of times, but for once, I couldn't speak.

'Oh!' Belle went on. 'Before I forget, the producers of *Honeydale* are throwing a party to mark the start of a new era on the soap. The team from *Star Secrets* have been invited – including you.'

'Oh, wow!' I said.

'Actually, the producer asked me to tell you that they were looking for some teenagers to be extras at Rosie Lynn's birthday party in an upcoming episode. He wondered if you and any of your friends would be interested. And in case you're worried, he's had a chat with Wendy about *her* attitude problem, too, so you won't get a frosty reception like the one I heard you got from her last time.'

'Interested?' I screeched. 'Do Girls Aloud wear short skirts? Of course I'm interested!'

'That's good,' Belle laughed down the phone. 'Cos I've already told him yes.'

I couldn't wait to see Abs's and Soph's faces. You know what? Having a mystery radar is totally coolisimo!

Fact File

NAME: Liz Parker
(Rosie's mum)

AGE: 37

STAR SIGN: Leo

HAIR: Brown

EYES: Brown

LOVES: Singing Bananarama songs and anything else to do with the 1980s

HATES: When she knows Rosie is up to something but won't tell her

LAST SEEN: On stage, singing in her Bananarama tribute band, the Banana Splits.

MOST LIKELY TO SAY: 'I just can't understand why nobody wears legwarmers anymore.'

WORST CRINGE EVER: When her leggings ripped during the Banana Splits' special performance at the local church hall. The vicar got the shock of his life!

School Cool

Don't let lessons get you down!
Try out the girls' boredom-busting tips!

calculator writing

If you turn your calculator upside down, some of the numbers look like letters. Try keying in 531608 Ha, ha, ha. Hours of fun!

Nifty notes

There's just no point passing notes in class. Teachers are totally wise to it. Instead, write on a plastic ruler with a felt pen. No teach will stop you from lending each other an innocent ruler. Genius!

Tap tennis

If you're truly bored, start up a game of tap tennis. One person taps their foot or a pen or whatever and the other player has to do a tap straight afterwards. Be subtle or you'll get caught. This game is what gets us through our drama lessons with Time Lord. It sounds silly but it's lots of fun!

All eyes

Any lesson is improved by sitting near a good-looking boy. Make an excuse to move your desk to a good viewing spot. If you don't have any boys in your school then you'll have to look at magazine pics of celeb boys underneath your desk instead!

Who's YOUR Star Secrets Fashion Twin?

Follow the flow to find your magazine style sister

Are you a total chatterbox? **NO** **YES**

NO

Do you like dressing up in crazy outfits?

YES

Do you prefer art lessons to English ones? **NO**

YES

Belle

 NO

Just like *Star Secrets* Editor Belle, you're always the first to try a new trend as soon as it hits the shops. You love offering style advice to your friends, who are usually grateful — especially when you lend them your fab accessories to make their outfits shine!

Are you addicted to chocolate?

YES

YES

Lauren

You and Lauren love to mix and match. Thanks to your awesome customising skills, you can look great on a budget, too. You've always got your eyes open for new ways to wear old stuff, and your wardrobe is simply bursting with gorgey bright colours!

Do you often wear bright colours?

NO

YES

Alice

Alice and you are like peas in a pod because you both know how to make jeans and trainers look très stylish! Whether you're wearing dark denim and a sparkly top, or baggy jeans and a sporty hooded top, you just don't feel like you if you're not in your jeans!

 **Are you good at customising your clothes?**

NO

Megastar

Everyone has blushing blunders - here are some from your Megastar Mystery friends!

Rosie

I ran out of things to do one day when I was working at *Star Secrets*, so I started writing an email to Abs and Soph about how cool everyone who works there is. I wrote loads about Pete, and how cute he looks when he brushes his hair out of his dark brown eyes when he's concentrating. He's so cute! Anyway, I guess I was thinking about him a little bit too hard as I sent it to him instead of to the girls! Sooo embarrassing!

Belle

I was running late for work as I had spent ages picking out a perfectly coordinating outfit. I ran as fast as I could in my heels to try and catch the bus, and I jumped on just before it drove away from the stop. But as the doors closed, my skirt got caught and I was trapped! It fluttered in the breeze as the bus drove along, and I was practically stuck to the door with my knickers on display. So not a good look!

Cringes

Sally

I had never been so excited (or nervous!) about my job as I was on my first day at *Honeydale*. My heart was pounding as the first actress sat down in the chair. I couldn't believe it – it was Cassie St Claire, the soap's biggest star! I picked up her favourite blue sparkly eyeliner and started to apply it but my jittery nerves got the better of me and I jabbed her in the eye! Ms St Claire screamed and leapt out of her seat, while I turned as red as a tomato!

Alice

I was at my mate Lizzie's house and we were mucking around, singing a Mirage Mullins song into the tape player I use to record interviews. The next day, I had a hot interview with Mirage herself! I turned my tape on but hit 'play' instead of 'record', and our terrible version of Mirage started blaring out through the interview room! Luckily Mirage saw the funny side, but I was bright red for the rest of the day!

The latest front cover of the mag always takes pride of place on her wall

Full-to-bursting contacts book, cos it's all about who you know, darling

What's your Super-sleuth Style?

Are you destined to be a detective like Rosie?
Answer the questions to find out!

1. Which of these would be your ideal present?

a. A book about star signs
b. Something homemade from your mates
c. The latest must-have gadget

2. Which of these nicknames would your friends be most likely to give you?

a. Magic, because sometimes it seems like you can read your mates' minds
b. Miss Mystery, because you're brilliant at getting to the bottom of things
c. Action Girl, because you're always in the middle of an adventure

3. What's your fave kind of movie?

a. Something knicker-wettingly spooky
b. You like mystery movies best
c. Films full of action and adventure are brill!

4. You never leave home without . . .

a. A big hat – you might need a last-minute disguise!
b. A camera – you never know when you might notice something out of the ordinary
c. Your mobile – texting your mates is an essential, not a luxury!

5. In class, you're most likely to be . . .

a. Investigating that awesomely juicy rumour you heard at playtime

b. Passing notes to your mates written in your own secret code

c. Desperately trying to finish last night's homework without your teacher noticing

6. Your style could be described as . . .

a. Mix 'n' match. You just chuck on whatever you find in the morning, and it usually looks great!

b. Pretty cool. Swapping accessories with your friends is your idea of heaven

c. Practical. You don't want loads of beads getting in your way when you're doing Kung Fu, do you?!

Mostly As: Starry-eyed Sister

You're really into horoscopes and have a true sixth sense whenever there's anything fishy going on. And you can normally solve problems in the wink of an eye, too!

Mostly Bs: Super-spy-in-the-making

Code-cracking and problem-solving always help you find out what's up. You love reading about mysteries and pick up loads of tips from your fave celeb sleuths!

Mostly Cs: Adventurous Angel

You and your gang of crime-busting friends make the ultimate team, since you've all got different skills to offer when you're in the middle of a mystery. They're lucky that they've got a leader as good as you!

Sally's On-set Secrets

TV make-up artists have all the insider info, and *Honeydale's* Sally has got loads to tell!

Shhh! None of the food in *Honeydale's* café is real! The ice cream is made from scoops of mash and the burgers are rubber. I found out the hard way by taking a sneaky bite of a choccy sundae on my first day. Cold mash – yuck!

Psst! Which glamorous *Honeydale* star's middle name is Gertrude? You're gonna have to guess, cos it's more than my job's worth to tell you!

Heads-up . . .

Take my advice and steer clear of the catering van. Unless you fancy a plate of liver curry, stinky sprout soup or deep-fried snails with mushy peas, that is!

It's a secret!

The bathrooms in *Honeydale* aren't real! Don't make the same mistake as one of the soap's biggest stars. He popped for a loo break between scenes, then found himself with a lot of explaining to do!

You'll never guess . . .

If you take a careful look in the background of the café scenes, you might spot yours truly having a good old natter to the costume lady over a cappuccino!

DIVA SPOTTING

Find out how to pick out (and avoid!) troublesome celebs with this handy guide

SUPER-BOUFFANT HAIR

Because she simply must look bigger and better than anyone else, darling

ANIMAL PRINT DRESS

She may look like a pussy cat, but she'll eat you for breakfast!

BIG RED LIPS

All the better for SHOUTING with!

LONG FINGERNAILS

For pointing dramatically at you while she calls out her orders

HIGH-HEELED BOOTS

Make an important-sounding clicking noise (and also warn you when she's coming!)

Soph's Style Tips

Writers never go anywhere without their trusty notebooks. Find out how to make a reporter's pad from a plain notepad here!

Tie a piece of string or ribbon round the clip of a pen lid, then tie the other end to the wire loops of your pad. Now you'll always have something to write with!

Write your name and your details on some brightly coloured paper, then cut it out and stick it on. Need an idea for a job title? Try 'Features Writer', 'Researcher' or even 'Editor'!

Rosie Parker
REPORTER
STAR SECRETS MAGAZINE

TOP SECRET

KEEP OUT

Keep nosy parkers out of your insider gossip by labelling your notebook 'Top Secret' and 'Keep Out!'. Then make sure you keep it hidden whenever you're not using it!

Stick pics of the stars you want to interview all over the cover for a showbiz touch!

Pam's Problem Page

Never fear, Pam's here to sort you out!

Dear Pam,

My boss is driving me mad! My job is to do her make-up, and every day she shouts at me for getting it wrong. I go home every night and practise a new look that I think she might like, but the next day she always says, 'That's awful! Can't you get anything right?'. It's making me so stressed out and unhappy!

Sally

Pam says: There, there, dear. I think I know exactly what will make you feel better. Have you tried having a nice sit-down in a comfy chair with a garibaldi or three instead of worrying about this silly woman? There's more to life than make-up, you know – Jessica Fletcher didn't get where she is today by worrying about her eyeshadow! If I were you, I'd tell your boss that as long as she always keeps herself neat and tidy, no one will think twice about the shade of her lipstick. Now, can I make you a good old cup of tea, love?

Can't wait for the next
book in the series?
Here's a sneak preview of

SongBird

Chapter One

My friend Soph is fashion obsessed. She's the only person I know who gets excited about going into charity shops. She spends most of the money from her Saturday job on the kind of hideous old clothes even your nan wouldn't wear. But Soph takes them home and somehow, through the amazing power of her scissors and sewing machine, turns them into utterly gorgey designer-type outfits. Which was why, when I found myself in the middle of a serious jumper-related crisis, she was the obvious person to ask for advice, along with my other best friend, Abs, who has a brain the size of a planet.

'Auntie Muriel sent me a present,' I told them. It was lunchtime and we were in the school canteen. 'An orange jumper with a totally huge and seriously disgusting yellow bunny on the front.'

'Stylish,' said Abs.

'The thing is, Mum won't let me take it back to the shop and change it for something – oh, I don't know – an earthling might wear. She says it's ungrateful.'

'Surely she doesn't expect you to wear it?' said Abs. 'She does know you're fourteen, right?'

'You wouldn't think so from the way she treats me sometimes,' I grouched.

Abs thought for a minute. 'Maybe you could dye it or something, and stick a piece of material over the rabbit?'

We looked at Soph. That sort of thing was totally her department.

'Er, Soph?' said Abs.

But she was completely vagued out, staring

across the canteen with a fork dangling from one hand. I followed the direction of her gaze, thinking maybe James Scott, this year-twelve boy who she has a humongous crush on, had just walked in. There was no sign of him though. In fact, unless Soph had developed a very recent thing for geeky comic-reading year sevens, there was no sign of anything interesting. Abs waggled her hand in front of Soph's face.

'What?' said Soph.

'We were just saying,' said Abs, 'about Rosie's bunny jumper.'

'What?' Soph practically shouted.

Suddenly, I twigged. Like the genius mystery-solver I am, I lifted up a big chunk of her wavy brown hair and saw exactly what I'd expected to see: an earpiece, attached to the tiny pink MP3 player Soph's dad had given her for getting an 'A' in Mr Footer's science test.

Honestly, Soph is sooo spoiled. I got an 'A' in English last term and all my mum said was, 'That's nice, love. Have you seen my legwarmers anywhere?' When I very patiently pointed out that proper parents – the kind who really love their daughters – buy presents as a reward for good grades, do you know what she said?

'I'll treat you to a chocolate-chip muffin next time we're in Trotters.'

Hours and hours of hard homeworky slog rewarded with a stingy bit of cake in an old person's café. I ask you.

I yanked the earpiece out of Soph's ear.

'Hey!' she protested.

'We're trying to have a conversation here, Soph,' I said.

'About clothes,' added Abs.

Soph frowned. You could practically see her brain whirring as she tried to work out whether sulking about the headphone thing was more important than sounding off on her specialist subject.

'What are you listening to that's so important anyway?' I asked, curious.

She pulled out the other earpiece and handed

one to Abs and one to me. I waited as Soph scrolled through the songs on her MP3 player.

'Here,' she said. 'Listen.'

'It's SongBird!' I said, recognising the tune straightaway.

'Who?' asked Abs.

'Exactly,' I said.

'Right,' said Abs. 'Great. Thanks for clearing that up for me.'

'SongBird,' I repeated. 'Haven't you seen the *MyPlace* webpage?'

Abs shook her head.

'My cousin sent me the link,' said Soph. 'The song's really cool, but I don't know anything about it except it's by SongBird.'

'*No one* knows anything about it,' I explained. 'It's this whole weird mystery. The song was posted on *MyPlace* a few weeks ago, but there's no picture on the page and no biog – just a name.'

'SongBird?' Abs suggested.

'Yep. And there's a message under the name that says, "I hope you enjoy listening to this as much as I enjoyed writing it", but that's all.'

'Weirdy beardy,' said Soph. 'Have you tried doing a search for it?'

'Do the French put garlic on their cornflakes?' I said. 'Mais oui. And not just me. Everyone wants to know who SongBird is. There's gossip all over the Internet about it.'

'What's the song called?' said Abs, listening to the earpiece again.

'"I Wish Things Were Different"' I said.

'*You can really do it, make a change. Oooh-oooh-oooh,*' sang Soph. She has a famously dreadful voice.

'If I'd written a song that good, there's no way I'd keep it quiet,' she said. 'Everyone would know it was me.'

Abs raised one of her eyebrows so high it disappeared under her fringe. 'Yep, they'd *definitely* know it was you, Soph,' she said.

Soph poked her tongue out.

'I don't think SongBird will be able to keep it quiet much longer,' I said.

Abs opened her yoghurt. 'How d'you mean?'

'Thousands of people have downloaded the song – probably hundreds of thousands by now. According to *Star Secrets* magazine, if it carries on like this, it'll soon be the most downloaded song ever.'

'That's a massivo secret to keep,' said Abs.

'Exactly,' I nodded. 'Someone's bound to find out who's behind it soon. Some nosy reporter, or maybe –'

I was about to suggest we could do some investigating ourselves, but before I could get the words out, there was a humongous crash and all three of us jumped. Soph shot a forkful of mashed potato across the table and Abs, who was still listening to the song, dropped the earpiece into her yoghurt. We whipped around to see a mousy-haired girl sitting at the end of our table, with a horrified expression on her face. She'd just knocked her tray off the table. It was upside down on the floor, along with her plate, knife, fork and a spreading pool of baked beans. Her uniform was covered in orange bean splatters that totally clashed with her red cheeks. What made me feel even worse was that it was Louise Collins. She's in the same form as me and Soph. Totally nice but, like, the quietest person I've *ever* met. Even more mousy than her hair, as Soph once said.

While we watched, Louise stood up, still looking horror-struck. Unfortunately, instead of calmly and quietly clearing up the mess, she caught her bag on the edge of the table. She stumbled backwards and this time sent her chair flying with another loud clatter. The canteen went loonissimo. Everyone turned round to stare, loads of people started laughing and there was even some clapping and cheering. Louise's face was seriously beetrooty.

'Could you be any clumsier, Colly-wobbles?' sneered a familiar voice from the next table. Amanda Hawkins: school witch and general evil-doer. Just when you thought things couldn't get any worse.

'Ignore her,' said Abs, quietly. I had this tendency to argue back with Amanda, which was never the best idea.

I didn't say anything, but went to help Louise pick up her lunch things.

'Thanks,' she said in a quiet, strangled kind of voice.

'Did you hear something?' said Amanda to her almost-as-evil cronies, Lara Neils and Keira Roberts. 'Eee-eee-eee, little mousy Colly-wobbles.' She made a squeaking noise and twitched her nose in what was supposed to be a mouse impression. How she gets all the best parts in school plays, I'll never know.

'Leave her alone, Amanda,' I said. I couldn't hold it in any longer.

'It's not my fault,' she said. 'I was minding my own business. She's the one who started crashing about, spoiling my lunch.'

'Yeah,' said Keira, sounding even dimmer than she looked.

'Y'know,' Amanda continued, 'I'm surprised. You wouldn't think a mouse like that *could* make more noise than a herd of stomping great elephants.'

Louise's face crumpled. Grabbing her bag, she ran out of the canteen.

'See you, loser!' Amanda called after her.

'That was totally hilarious,' said Lara.

'Well funny,' agreed Keira.

'Are you three sharing one brain cell today?' I said, finally snapping. 'What's funny about making someone cry?'

'I'll show you, if you like,' Amanda threatened.

'As if,' said Abs.

'Oooh, Four-eyes is getting narky now,' said Amanda. Apart from being an evil witch, she's totally thick, too. Abs wasn't even wearing her glasses.

'It must be hard,' I said in a loud voice to Abs and Soph, 'being so utterly boring, your only hobby is picking on people. You have to feel sorry for her.'

'You'll be feeling sorry if you don't shut up,' said Amanda.

I was just about to answer when I spotted Mrs Oldham (English teacher, deputy head and famous shouter) striding in through the canteen doors.

Even though I was still fuming, I knew there was no point carrying on with the argument. Mrs Oldham may have the dress sense of a line-dancer, but she has the eyes of a hawk and the nose of a police sniffer dog. She'd be over at the first sign of an argument and, knowing Amanda Hawkins like I unfortunately do, she'd sooo manage to twist things and make it all look like my fault.

No way was she having the last word, though.

'D'you want to come over here and say that?' I said.

Massivo cliché, but that stuff works on a halfwit like Amanda.

She stood up and stepped over to our table. 'Maybe I do.'

'Uh-oh,' said Abs, realising what I was up to. 'Oldham's just walked in.'

Amanda spun round and saw Mrs O looking straight at us. She quickly sat down in the seat opposite.

'I think it's time we left,' I said.

'Absolutely,' said Abs.

'OK,' said Soph, who looked a bit confused.

'Nosy, Four-eyes and the Fashion Freak,' Amanda called after us. 'You lot deserve each other.'

'That chair Amanda just sat on,' said Soph as we stacked our trays by the door, 'wasn't it . . .'

'Yep,' I grinned. 'The one your mashed potato landed on.'

* * *

It's amazing how seeing a girl walk round with mashed potato on her bum all afternoon can cheer you up. Amanda Hawkins was still a complete troll, but I saw Louise by her locker just before the afternoon bell rang and she looked a bit more cheerful. She'd changed out of the bean-splattered uniform into her gym kit and her face was back to its normal colour. She gave me a small smile as she hurried past.

In fact, the only bit I found myself thinking about when I got home was the idea that we could try to find out who SongBird really was. After all, we'd solved plenty of mysteries before and this one was really interesting. Like Soph said, why would anyone want to keep quiet about writing such a cool song?

I was just thinking it over when my phone beeped. It was a text from Abs:

Turn on MTV now!

By some miracle, my Nan, who is dangerously television obsessed – murder-mystery shows in particular – was out at Trotter's, so I didn't have to wrestle her for the remote control. I flipped through a couple of channels before I found the right one. And there it was, halfway through the second verse – 'I Wish Things Were Different'. I sat with my mouth open. It was definitely SongBird – I'd listened to it so many times, I'd recognise her voice anywhere – but she didn't look anything like I'd imagined. She was seriously gorgeous – tall and thin with short, wavy blonde hair and bright green eyes. She looked more like a model than a singer. The video wasn't brilliant – lots of shaky close-ups and SongBird smiling into the camera. It had obviously been done in a real rush, which made sense, considering the mystery behind it. There was something a bit odd about it all, though. When the song finished, I switched the TV off and went upstairs.

I'd visited SongBird's *MyPlace* page so often, I didn't need to look up the address. Now, instead of the almost-blank screen, there was a photo of the girl from the video, a biog and a name: Georgina Good. I scrolled down to the biog, itching to find out more about her.

Hi! It's brilliant to be able to add my pic and real name to the website at last. I'm really happy that so many people like my song. I've been writing music and singing for ages. 'I Wish Things Were Different' is about how we can all make a difference if we want to. It's good to be a bit mysterious, which is why I've been so secretive until now. See you on tour!

So that was that. I flopped back on to my bed, feeling kind of disappointed. It looked like there was no mystery for us to solve after all.